DATE DUE		
JAN 0 2 2019		
NOV 2 9 2019		

3YZJR000275025
Ione, Larissa   37325
Hawkyn
SCF ION $9.99

Hawkyn

Also from Larissa Ione

Hawkyn

A Demonica Underworld Novella

By Larissa Ione

1001 Dark Nights

EVIL EYE
CONCEPTS

Hawkyn
A Demonica Underworld Novella
By Larissa Ione

1001 Dark Nights

Copyright 2018 Larissa Ione
ISBN: 978-1-945920-95-0

Forward: Copyright 2014 M. J. Rose

Published by Evil Eye Concepts, Incorporated

Acknowledgments from the Author

I just want to send out a continued thank you to all my readers who have been so patient as I wrap up three years of personal life matters that meant a much, much reduced writing schedule. As we finish up the house we've been building and get moved into it, I expect my writing pace to pick up. I'm excited about what the future is going to bring, and I hope you are too!

Sign up for the 1001 Dark Nights Newsletter
and be entered to win a Tiffany Key necklace.

There's a contest every month!

Go to www.1001DarkNights.com to subscribe.

As a bonus, all subscribers will receive a free copy of
Discovery Bundle Three
Featuring stories by
Sidney Bristol, Darcy Burke, T. Gephart
Stacey Kennedy, Adriana Locke
JB Salsbury, and Erika Wilde

One Thousand and One Dark Nights

Once upon a time, in the future...

*I was a student fascinated with stories and learning.
I studied philosophy, poetry, history, the occult, and
the art and science of love and magic. I had a vast
library at my father's home and collected thousands
of volumes of fantastic tales.*

*I learned all about ancient races and bygone
times. About myths and legends and dreams of all
people through the millennium. And the more I read
the stronger my imagination grew until I discovered
that I was able to travel into the stories... to actually
become part of them.*

*I wish I could say that I listened to my teacher
and respected my gift, as I ought to have. If I had, I
would not be telling you this tale now.
But I was foolhardy and confused, showing off
with bravery.*

*One afternoon, curious about the myth of the
Arabian Nights, I traveled back to ancient Persia to
see for myself if it was true that every day Shahryar
(Persian: شهريار, "king") married a new virgin, and then
sent yesterday's wife to be beheaded. It was written
and I had read, that by the time he met Scheherazade,
the vizier's daughter, he'd killed one thousand
women.*

Something went wrong with my efforts. I arrived in the midst of the story and somehow exchanged places with Scheherazade – a phenomena that had never occurred before and that still to this day, I cannot explain.

Now I am trapped in that ancient past. I have taken on Scheherazade's life and the only way I can protect myself and stay alive is to do what she did to protect herself and stay alive.

Every night the King calls for me and listens as I spin tales. And when the evening ends and dawn breaks, I stop at a point that leaves him breathless and yearning for more. And so the King spares my life for one more day, so that he might hear the rest of my dark tale.

As soon as I finish a story... I begin a new one... like the one that you, dear reader, have before you now.

GLOSSARY

The Aegis—Society of human warriors dedicated to protecting the world from evil. Recent dissension among its ranks reduced its numbers and sent The Aegis in a new direction.

Fallen Angel—Believed to be evil by most humans, fallen angels can be grouped into two categories: True Fallen and Unfallen. Unfallen angels have been cast from Heaven and are earthbound, living a life in which they are neither truly good nor truly evil. In this state, they can, rarely, earn their way back into Heaven. Or they can choose to enter Sheoul, the demon realm, in order to complete their fall and become True Fallens.

Harrowgate—Vertical portals, invisible to humans, used to travel between locations on Earth and Sheoul. A very few beings can summon their own personal Harrowgates.

Inner Sanctum—A realm within Sheoul-gra that consists of five Rings, each housing the souls of demons categorized by their level of evil as defined by the Ufelskala. The Inner Sanctum is run by the fallen angel Hades and his staff of wardens, all fallen angels. Access to the Inner Sanctum is strictly limited, as the demons imprisoned within can take advantage of any outside object or living person in order to escape.

Memitim—Earthbound angels assigned to protect important humans called Primori. Memitim remain earthbound until they complete their duties, at which time they Ascend, earning their wings and entry into Heaven.

Primori—Humans and demons whose lives are fated to affect the world in some crucial way.

Sheoul—Demon realm some call Hell. Located on its own plane deep in the bowels of the Earth, accessible to most only by Harrowgates and hellmouths.

Sheoul-gra—A realm that exists independently of Sheoul, it is overseen by Azagoth, also known as the Grim Reaper. Within Sheoul-gra is the Inner Sanctum, where demon souls go to be kept in torturous limbo until they can be reborn.

Shrowd—When angels travel through time, they exist within an impenetrable bubble known as a shrowd. While in the shrowd, angels are invisible and cannot interact with anyone—human, demon, or angel—outside the shrowd. Breaking out of the shrowd is a serious transgression that can, and has, resulted in execution. Also called a *quantamun*.

Ufelskala—A scoring system for demons, based on their degree of evil. All supernatural creatures and evil humans can be categorized into the five Tiers, with the Fifth Tier comprising the worst of the wicked.

Chapter One

"Ha! I made you bleed, you worm."

Hawkyn glared at his opponent as he dabbed the back of his hand against his mouth and came away with blood. Yup, Cipher had given him a split lip, all right, and he cursed as Razr, their sparring coach, ticked off a point for Ciph.

Cursing again, Hawkyn launched at his blond Unfallen angel buddy, landing a heel-first kick in the guy's gut. As an Unfallen, an angel who had been kicked out of Heaven but hadn't completed his fall, Cipher didn't have the powers of either a True Fallen angel or a Heavenly angel, but somehow, he still managed to be a powerful force.

The bastard.

"Point to Hawk," Razr called out. "It's a tie match. Take a break, you two. We'll start round three in fifteen minutes." Razr shot Hawkyn one of his signature I'm-a-dick smiles. "Maybe you can finally pull your head out of your ass and win a match."

"Yeah, yeah," Hawkyn muttered. "I didn't get enough sleep last night."

Cipher reached for his bottle of water on the nearby bench as Razr headed toward another pair of sparring opponents who, like Hawkyn and Cipher, were clad in black sweatpants and white tees that showed every drop of blood and sweat.

"Don't tell me you finally got laid?"

"Hardly. You know the law." Hawkyn hadn't felt the erotic touch of a female in hundreds of years, and even then, sex had been more of a momentary escape from a shitty existence than something meaningful or even nice.

But that had been back before he'd been ripped from the human world and thrust into the angelic one, the one in which Memitim had to swear an oath to celibacy. Supposedly, abstinence made warriors more dangerous. The demon Hawkyn had killed just yesterday would probably agree.

Son of a bitch, he was horny. If he didn't earn his wings soon to free himself from the idiotic rules Memitim had to follow—including celibacy—he was going to explode. Sometimes he thought that the Memitim who had never had sex had it better, because once you knew what you were missing...

"So what kept you up?" Cipher poured water on his head and shook it off, his blond hair, longer and two shades darker than Hawkyn's, flinging a rain of droplets like a dog after a bath.

"The newest Star Trek series. Have you seen it?" It was a lie, but he wasn't ready to share the truth with Cipher. The guy was his best friend, but Cipher didn't fully understand Memitim business and didn't seem to want to learn it. What he did know he seemed to have absorbed via osmosis or some shit.

"Star Trek?" Cipher scoffed. "A new Star Wars series would be worth losing a sparring match over, but Trek? No way."

Hawkyn laughed. "Did I tell you I was Nimoy's Memitim guardian back in the sixties? And you know my brother Reynaud. He was Shatner's. Linsef was Nichelle Nichols'."

"What? You're kidding. The actors were Primori? They needed to be protected? From what? The Gorn?" Cipher laughed. Hard. He always thought his jokes were funny.

The Gorn were no laughing matter. Lizard warriors. Hardcore.

"Dude, Star Trek played a role in history," Hawk shot back. "The vital people involved, starting at the top with Gene Roddenberry, were all watched over."

"Hey, boys. What's going on?" Suzanne, Hawk's younger sister— by a few centuries—stopped near the bench, her wavy brown hair pulled back in a headband, her arms full of yellow squash from the nearby garden. All Memitim who lived here had jobs in order to keep the place running, and Suzanne had been assigned as cook. Hell, she'd begged to take shifts in the kitchen.

Hawkyn gestured to Cipher. "This fool is trying to convince me that Star Wars is better than Star Trek."

"It is," Cipher said. "And not just better. More popular. I'll bet Han Solo is more recognized around the world than Spock is."

Blasphemy. Hawkyn threw up his hands in disgust. "You're delusional. Even if you're right, *and you're not*, Star Trek definitely had a much bigger impact on human society than Star Wars. An interracial kiss seen around the world. Communicators inspired cell phone design. Medical equipment got a boost from Star Trek's diagnostic beds and scanners."

Cipher rolled his eyes. "It's called technology. Humanity would have come up with that stuff eventually."

"Yeah?" Hawk wiped sweat off his brow. "I haven't seen NASA name a space shuttle after the Millennium Falcon."

"Okay, guys." Suzanne attempted to wave her hands in a time-out gesture but nearly lost her load of veggies. "Knock it off. I have a question for you, Hawk."

"Whatcha got?"

She juggled with her squash as she turned over her right arm to expose the single, circular Primori mark, a *heraldi*, on the inside of her wrist.

"Declan's mark keeps alerting me to danger," she said, "but when I flash to him, there's nothing happening. I've waited for hours for the alert to shut off, I've searched all over his immediate vicinity for any kind of threat, from human snipers to demon assassins, and there's been nothing. I've heard that sometimes our very first *heraldis* can be glitchy. Do you think that's what's happening?"

"My first one was glitchy too," Hawk said. "My sponsor said it can take our bodies a while to adjust to being in tune with another person." His had taken a couple of years, which was why a Memitim's first Primori was often their only Primori for the first five years.

"Do they ever fail to notify us when our Primori is in trouble?"

"Yup." He caught a squash that escaped her arms. "Our sister Nephritt lost her very first Primori when his *heraldi* didn't alert her that he was in danger."

Suzanne's brown doe eyes shot wide. "That's terrifying. Maybe I should check on Declan more often."

"I get the feeling you check on him enough," Hawkyn said as he placed the gourd on the top of her squash pile.

She blushed, which told him he'd hit the mark. He'd seen the way she looked at the human she was assigned to watch over. It was as if she had been trapped in the Inner Sanctum's 5th Ring's scorch pit for a week and he was carrying a glass of water. And a thousand-foot ladder.

"He's my first," she said with a stubborn sniff, her nose in the air. "And I'm going to make sure I do my job right."

"That's the problem," he said, hoping he didn't come off as too lecture-happy. Suzanne would tune out faster than a *griminion* could reap a soul. "You're *not* doing your job right. We aren't supposed to interact with our Primori or the people around them. We're supposed to watch from a distance or from the invisibility of the *shrowd*. But you've been hanging out at the restaurant where he works and chatting up his friends and co-workers."

"Declan doesn't work at Top," she shot back, getting prickly. "He works for the restaurant owner's brother at McKay-Taggart, and their families and employees are kind of intertwined, so he's there a lot. And I just happen to like the food. Plus, there are a surprising number of Primori associated with both Top and McKay-Taggart, so I'm doing my brothers and sisters a favor by keeping an eye on their charges. And I've gotten some great contacts that could help me take my cooking show to a whole new level." She spun on her tennis shoe-clad foot and started toward the main dormitory building, which housed Sheoul-gra's largest of several kitchens. "Now, if you'll excuse me," she called out as she walked, "I have to start on dinner before I get too annoyed."

No, no one wanted her to cook while she was annoyed. Her moods infused the food she prepared, so a happy Suzanne was a recipe for happy diners. Not to mention the fact that her food was extra delicious when she was enjoying herself, which was almost always. She took her job as a cook as seriously as she took her job as a guardian, although she certainly didn't look at that squash the way she did the human she was watching over.

"I worry about her," he said to Cipher after she was out of earshot. "She's not ready to have a Primori. Hell, she's not suited for this shit at all."

Cipher snorted. "Dude, I've sparred with her. She's an awesome fighter. She moves like a damned snake. She's way faster than I am."

Cipher must be really impressed, because he never admitted that anyone was better in any way than he was. And he was usually right. He was a tough bastard whose fighting skills made him one of the most sought-after trainers in Sheoul-gra. The challenge was getting him away from his computer. The guy's cyber-skills were on par with his fighting skills.

"It's not her fighting ability that concerns me," Hawkyn sighed. "It's her innocence. She's so naïve."

"She's had decades of exposure to underworld shit and demons, hasn't she?"

"Yes, but it's humans I worry about." He watched Suz disappear into the building.

"Humans?" Cipher barked out a laugh. "Humans are freaking harmless."

He glanced over at his buddy. Cipher was a little naïve, too. "She didn't grow up like most Memitim. She had a good life."

Cipher's voice was flat. "Oh, the horror."

"You don't get it." Hawk swiped his water bottle from the bench. "Memitim infants are intentionally put into shitty situations. Bad parents, war zones, poverty... It's to challenge us as we grow up."

"Sounds like it could turn you into a bunch of psychos," Cipher mused as he went for his own water. "Explains a lot, actually."

No argument there. A lot of Hawk's brothers and sisters had serious issues, and Suzanne could often be found trying to fix them. Usually with food.

"Yeah, well, Suz somehow ended up with a near perfect life. Loving family, popular in school, lots of friends. Chipped nails were the worst things that ever happened to her. She didn't really date, didn't get into a lot of trouble. She lived in fucking Pleasantville. Then she went straight from an idyllic human life to the Memitim training center in Hawaii, which is pretty much a spa."

Hawkyn had been assigned to the facility in Belgium, a cold-ass castle with strict rules. Yes, he could have lived on his own after his fifty years of mandatory fledgling training was complete, but he'd chosen to stay...until Sheoul-gra unexpectedly opened up to Memitim a couple of years ago.

Well, it had always been open to Memitim who wanted to serve Azagoth, but Sheoul-gra had been a dark, grim, horrible place where few wanted to be until Azagoth's mate, Lilliana, came along. Now it was teeming with life and activity and a thriving community of Memitim, Unfallen angels, and even a few Fallen angels.

"So she hasn't seen what humans are capable of," Cipher mused.

"Exactly. She hasn't been hurt. And I see her getting too attached to her Primori."

"You're her sponsor. Can't you talk to the Memitim embassy and get her reassigned?"

Hawkyn barked out a laugh. "I don't know why I even tried. Got the standard 'Primori are assigned to specific Memitim for a reason' bullshit."

"I heard you can ask for one reassignment per century." Cipher drained his water bottle in half a dozen swallows and tossed it to the ground for one of the new trainees to pick up. There were few trash bins in training areas for a reason, and as far as Hawk could tell, that reason was to make trainees hate life. "You ever try to get one of your Primori reassigned?"

"Nope. Never." Hawkyn had been assigned a lot of brutal scumbags in his hundreds of years of service, and he'd managed just fine.

"Razr's coming back." Cipher jerked his head in the other fallen angel's direction. "Better get your head on straight or I'm gonna kick your ass again."

Hawk snorted. "I was just warming up. Prepare for a beating." And then after he knocked Cipher around, he was going to pay his least favorite Primori a visit and fantasize about doing the same to him.

Someday, he swore silently. *Someday.*

* * * *

The best thing about grocery shopping at midnight was that the stores were relatively quiet. As someone sensitive to life-force energy, Aurora Mercer liked that. But sometimes the lack of activity wasn't a good thing.

Like now, as she walked her groceries out to her car. Fog common to Portland, Oregon in the fall had rolled in, obscuring everything farther than about forty feet out. She'd parked her dark blue Mercedes close to the building and under a light, but as she opened the rear door she was unnerved to see a black van pull next to her, blocking her faint view of the store—and blocking employee views of her.

The van's windows were blacked out.

She laughed nervously. It was probably nothing. Serial killers didn't drive anything so obvious, right?

Right?

Still, she picked up her pace, not caring that she was all but throwing her groceries in the back seat and food was spilling everywhere. She could salvage the cherries on the floor when she got home, and raspberry juice stains on cream leather wouldn't look *that* bad.

Not as bad as blood.

She finished and slammed the door closed. But shit...the cart corral was several stalls away. Her heart started racing at the thought of getting that far from her car and the light. Screw it, she could leave the cart here. She hated when people did that, but avoiding death was as good an excuse as any to be lazy.

Hastily she pushed the cart in front of her car, secured it over a concrete tire block—

"Fog's bad, isn't it?"

She spun around with a startled yelp. An attractive man, maybe six-four with a Celtic cross tattoo on his neck, stood between her and her driver side door. How had he gotten there so fast?

Stay calm.

Easier said than done, but she'd give it a shot. "Excuse me," she said firmly. "I'm in a hurry."

He didn't budge. "I'm sure you are."

As casually as she could, she reached into her purse for her keys and the attached canister of pepper spray, but as she fished around she realized she'd left them on her back seat. Her heart skipped a beat and then pounded so fast and hard she could feel it in her ears.

Deep breaths. You don't have your pepper spray, but you aren't weaponless.

The man smiled as if he knew she'd come up empty of pepper spray and was happy about it. "Problem? Something I can help you with?"

"No. Thank you." She dredged up a smile of her own and prayed it looked genuine and not like she was scared out of her mind. "If you'll step aside, I'll just go—"

She broke off as, out of the corner of her eye, she detected movement. Another man-shaped shadow stepped out of the fog behind the van, and her throat constricted with terror.

Jesus, there's two of them.

Never before had she used her abilities in an emergency. She'd always wondered if she even *could* use them. What if she froze in the face of danger? But now, as adrenaline careened through her body, she drew on the ancient magic, and with a single word, "maleseum," she struck out with her most powerful weapon, one her people usually reserved for only non-humans, like demons.

An intense, almost overwhelming pulse of ecstasy rocked her from inside out, triggered by the activation of magic. It was a curse— or gift—of her species, one that required them to either release their energy through sex or magic, but either way, the result was pleasure, even, apparently, during life or death situations.

Through the haze of the *morgasm*, as many of her friends called it, a bar of searing light blasted from her palm, striking the newcomer like a sledgehammer. He flew backward into a light pole and crumpled to the asphalt with a sickening thud. But in the time it took to neutralize the second man, the first moved on her. Pain shattered her face as his fist cracked against her jaw. The parking lot spun as she wheeled around and then hit the ground hard.

Despite the pain and the screaming inside her own head she heard him mutter something like "Thank you for that" as he looped some sort of rope or cord around her neck. She gasped for air, clawing at her throat, aware that he was dragging her toward his vehicle.

Terror fueled her fight as she kicked wildly, but her attacker was strong and she couldn't stop him from throwing her through the side door of his van. She landed hard on a metal floor, and before she could even process the fact that her vision was dimming, she felt a blow that put her into complete oblivion.

Her last thought before she lost consciousness was that she would have been home right now if she hadn't spent that extra ten minutes debating between Cheerios and Frosted Flakes.

Chapter Two

Hawkyn groaned as he opened his eyes, the stench of charred flesh rousing him to consciousness.

He must have been struck by a bus. Or a bomb. Had to be. As his vision cleared he realized he was in a parking lot, laid out at the base of a light pole, and it all came back to him.

He'd made a split-second decision that was probably a huge mistake.

He'd flashed to one of his Primori's locations and, in an instinctive reaction, had tried to interfere in a woman's abduction, something that was against Memitim rules. And he'd paid for it. But dammit, the pretty blonde had looked afraid and helpless, and he'd known full well what the owner of the van was going to do to her.

But she'd clearly not been as defenseless as Hawk had thought. No, she'd had a trick up her sleeve. A trick powerful enough to damage an angel. Which meant she was either not human or she was a human who possessed the kind of magic that could be wielded by very few. Maybe a demon-slaying member of The Aegis or an investigator with the Demonic Activity Response Team. She could also be a witch or possessed by a demon.

Interesting.

He eyed her car, remembering the terror in her face as she was dragged toward the van. Hawk had attempted to help even after she'd blasted him, but she'd left him paralyzed, unable to do more than wiggle his fingers. Hell, it had taken as much effort as he could muster to even remain conscious for as long as he had.

Headlights from an approaching car cut through the thick fog and blinded him, reminding him that he was still on the ground, in public, smoke wafting from a searing chest wound. Pain ripped through him as he struggled to his feet. He needed to see a healer, and fast. Whatever the female had zapped him with wasn't healing as rapidly as it should, and anything that powerful could continue to cause damage until the magic was neutralized.

Clutching his charred rib cage, he limped over to the female's car and checked for ID, but the bastard must have taken her purse. The vehicle registration, however, indicated that the Mercedes belonged to an Aurora Mercer. Okay, now what? He'd interfered with fate by trying to keep her out of the man's clutches... But had her fate been to be captured, or would she have used her weapon on her attacker instead of Hawkyn?

Shit. He was going to have to fix this, and fast.

But right now, he needed medical attention. He just hoped Aurora didn't need it as badly as he did.

* * * *

Faintly, somewhere in the distance, a rooster crowed.

A rooster? Usually it was the neighbor's yappy dog that woke Aurora in the mornings. She wasn't in her bed at home, was she?

Pain and cobwebs in her brain left her confused and panicked as she opened her eyes. Then shit got a whole lot worse.

She'd come to in what appeared to be a giant metal room, a box, maybe, lit by a single, dim bulb hanging by a cord from the metal ceiling. Along one wall was a wheeled table, the objects on top of it concealed by a sheet. Was this a shipping container? Or a train car? Didn't matter, she supposed, and thinking too hard about it only made her head throb more. She tasted blood, and as she raised her hand to test her swollen jaw, chains rattled.

Wincing, she looked down at the shackles around her wrists and ankles. The connected chains had been attached to hefty anchors in the metal supports in the wall.

Oh, God. Deep inside her chest, fear made her heart cower so completely she swore it was pressing against her spine.

But hey, at least she had a moldy, stained mattress to lie on, and her abductor had left her water. In a dog bowl. There was another bowl too, for going to the bathroom she assumed, given the partial roll of toilet paper next to it. How thoughtful.

Shit, she was in trouble.

Closing her eyes, she reached deep for her powers, but the empty tingle she felt in her chest was as she'd feared; she'd blown her entire wad on the one man in the parking lot, leaving nothing for the second.

How many times had her parents warned her about keeping a cool head in times of crisis? Her people had been warriors since the day their creator had crossed a male human witch with a succubus who drained humans of their energy and life force. But Aurora had turned her back on that history. Had fancied herself a rebel...which was also a hallmark of her species.

Their creator had attempted to harness their power for his own sadistic purposes, using them as soldiers in his bid to wrest power away from the rulers of ancient human empires. But Aurora's people had rebelled, killing him and his associates, and then they'd spread out, living among humans. Mating with them. Practically becoming them.

And now, because she'd embraced humanity and forsaken her warrior background, she was probably going to die a slow, torturous death, just as her annoying Navy SEAL brother had warned her. He'd tried to prepare her, to make it clear that one should hone every skill they had at their disposal, and that her stubborn refusal to use magic would fail her someday.

She hated that he was right. She could practically hear Aaron at her funeral already.

"I tried to tell her. Take some self-defense classes. Practice your magic. Build your stamina. Maintain situational awareness. But no, she would rather live and die as a human than embrace what made her special. And now I have to take time out of my day for her funeral."

Okay, so he wasn't *that* callous. But still. He'd be so disappointed in her.

The sound of footsteps outside scared her out of the glib thoughts she shouldn't be wasting her time with. Aaron would, no doubt, have spent his time plotting an escape. She'd just disappointed him yet again.

Truth be told, she'd disappointed herself, too.

Metal clanged, and terror made even her organs quiver as the container door rattled open. Through the narrow opening, the man from the parking lot stepped inside.

The darkness from outside seemed to spill in with him. His tennis shoes thudded ominously as he moved toward her, one corner of his mouth twisted into an evil smirk.

"Hi, Aurora," he said, almost pleasantly, as if he was welcoming her into his home.

Making things even more disturbing, he didn't look like a monster. His clean cut reddish hair and glasses gave him a non-threatening appearance, and his dad jeans and kelly green polo shirt completed the nerdy, I'm-a-friendly-dude look. He was Jack the Ripper in Dexter clothing.

She didn't reply, but then, he probably didn't expect her to.

"Aren't you curious about how I know your name?" he asked.

"I assume you went through my purse."

"Oh, honey, you're smart for a masseuse." He moved closer, just a couple of steps, and her pulse kicked up a notch. "I'm Jason. Jason Drayger." Still so pleasant. She wondered if he'd be as nice while he was slicing her up. "Can I do anything to make your stay more comfortable?"

She held up her wrists. "Keys would be great."

"I think we both know that won't be happening."

Of course not. But she had to keep her head on straight. Play along to buy time to plot. She wasn't dumb enough to think she could charm the bastard into letting her go, but if she could get her hands on him, she could absorb his energy, refill her well, and use it to escape.

"Could you at least loosen the shackles, Mr. Drayger?"

He leveled her a *nice try* look. "That won't be happening, either."

"Then why did you ask if you could do anything to make me more comfortable?"

"Just getting your hopes up, I guess."

"What hopes?"

"That you'll make it out of here alive."

His chilling words made her gut turn over in a violent somersault. She'd known she was in trouble and was going to die. But to hear him say it, to hear him toy with her, was too much to handle and she had to swallow over and over to keep from throwing up.

"What are you going to do to me?" she croaked, the effort of keeping her dinner down making her voice rough.

"I figured you'd ask that. They all do." He lifted one corner of the sheet covering the table and picked up a photo album. He blew dust off the surface and tossed it onto the mattress next to her.

Don't look. Do. Not. Look.

She knew she shouldn't, especially given the creepy anticipatory gleam in Drayger's dead, pale blue eyes, but she flipped open the cover anyway.

She instantly wished she hadn't.

Horror filled her mouth with bile and her stomach heaved again. That poor woman.

She shoved the album away so hard it landed on the floor, spilling more gruesome photos of several women from its tattered covers.

"Forty-one in all," he said, gesturing to the album. "Plus five I didn't take pictures of. With the first ones, you're finding yourself, you know? Trying to get your shit together. Figuring out what works and what doesn't. Plus, all that adrenaline is flowing through you, and you're not thinking straight." He smiled wistfully. "But I've got it down to a science now. I'll just leave that album with you so you can see what's in your future."

"You sick fuck," she rasped. "You evil bastard." *Forty-six women?* How had he not been caught yet?

"Me? Evil?" He snorted. "Let's talk about whatever dark magic *you* possess. Or are you going to deny what you did in the parking lot?"

"Deny?" That would be pointless, since he clearly had witnessed the power flowing from her fingertips. "No," she spat. "In fact, I'd do it again. I just hope your buddy suffered before he died."

Drayger's sharp laughter echoed off the walls. "That guy you blasted wasn't my friend. I have no idea who he was. You whacked some Good Samaritan who was probably trying to help you."

She felt the blood drain from her face. "Oh, my God," she whispered. "Oh, Jesus."

Drayger snarled. "Don't you invoke His name. He won't help you, witch." He moved closer, his amiable demeanor turned into something twisted and ugly that matched his insides. "I've dealt with your kind before, you know. My mom would do...things. She taught me to recognize your evil."

Aurora's mind was still spinning with the knowledge that she'd killed some innocent human, but somehow she had to stay on topic.

To ask questions that might help her later.

"Are...are all the women in your book..."

"They were all evil users of magic." He spat on the floor as if just talking about magic disgusted him. "Demons, some of them. Or shapeshifters. Mostly human witches, though."

"So that's why you chose me?" Shock rippled through her. She'd been so careful when it came to using her abilities. "Have you been stalking me?"

"Know what's crazy?" he asked, and she bit her tongue before she blurted the obvious answer of "You." "It was pure dumb luck that I found you. I stopped at the grocery store for milk, and there you were, radiating an unnatural aura like a neon sign."

God, it was no wonder he hadn't been caught yet. Profilers were probably driving themselves insane trying to figure out what his victims had in common, and unless someone working on the case was aware of the underworld, supernatural powers as a commonality wouldn't occur to them.

He lifted the hem of his shirt to reveal a leather sheath strapped to his abs, a knife handle protruding from it, and her heart leaped into her throat. He slid the blade free and flipped it in his hand with practiced precision that made her skin crawl.

"Now, don't worry," he said as he tested the edge of the knife. "I'm not going to kill you right away. We have days of foreplay ahead of us. Tonight is just going to be a taste."

Inside her head she started to scream, knowing that the real screams would start soon enough.

Chapter Three

"Dude. That's fucked up. Does it hurt?"

"What," Hawkyn gritted out, his breath coming in shallow pants, "this gaping hole in my chest? Yeah. Stings a little."

Clad in green scrubs, Darien, Hawkyn's ebony-haired half-brother and Sheoul-gra's resident healer, gestured to a chair in his office. "Did you at least save your Primori?"

It was pretty safe to assume that any injured Memitim had taken the damage during a battle to protect their Primori, and Hawk was perfectly okay with letting Darien believe that was true in this case. All of the thousands of Memitim were Hawkyn's brothers and sisters, sired by the same male, but functionally they were no different than anyone in the general population, stabbing each other in the back, fighting, and being assholes. Hawkyn trusted few Memitim, and Darien wasn't one of them.

"My Primori is fine," he said, which was true.

"How about the guy who did this to you?"

"It was a female. And I don't know." An image of her, helpless and afraid, filled him with guilt as he peeled off his ruined shirt and sank into the hard plastic chair. He'd seen so much ugliness in his centuries of life, but for some reason, this was affecting him more than usual. But he wasn't going to be able to do anything about it if he didn't take care of his injuries. "So, can you fix me, or what?"

Darien's skeptical expression was all Hawk needed as answer. "I'm best with non-magical injuries. If you'd been eviscerated with a sword, it'd be right up my alley." He kneeled next to Hawkyn with a tiny vial of glowing green liquid. "This might work, but I need to know what kind of demon did this to you."

"I have no idea. She vibed human." A human who was, no doubt, suffering right now.

"A witch, then? An Aegi?"

"Dunno. Maybe." At Darien's huff of annoyance, Hawkyn gave one of his own. "So, can you fix me?" he repeated.

"I told you, I'm better with injuries of non-magical origin."

"That's not very helpful."

"You know what's not helpful?" Darien gestured to Hawkyn's charred wound. "Your inability to identify the type of weapon that injured you."

"Don't know what to tell you. The female blasted me with some sort of silver-blue light. Next thing I knew, I was waking up in a pile of smoking flesh."

Darien's fingers smoothed over the edges of the wound, and Hawkyn hissed in pain. "It's partially healed. How long were you out?"

"I don't know. Maybe an hour."

"Damn." Darien frowned. "It should have healed more than this."

Duh. "Which is why I'm here."

"Okay." Darien held up the vial and popped off the rubber stopper. "I'm going to try this elixir on it. It's good for a lot of the kinds of spells human witches use."

"I don't think it was a spell. It seemed innate and organic." Spells cast by humans were often preceded by a warning tingle Hawkyn could feel like tiny pinpricks on his scalp, but abilities that were species traits usually gave no detectible warning, which was damned inconvenient.

Darien's hand paused with the dropper hovering over the pulsing gash. "Then...there might be some wee side effects."

"What kind of side effects?" It was a safe bet that Darien wasn't talking about dry mouth, blurred vision, or anal leakage.

"Depends on the species of the person who wielded the power. And the power itself, of course."

That didn't sound good. Hawkyn narrowed his eyes at the healer. "Examples?"

"Well, I once used it on a strange blister that formed on Llewellyn's arm after a Thraycer demon battle. The elixir caused blisters to erupt all over his body. You don't want to know what came out of them." Darien's brown eyes glittered with excitement. He had always gotten a kick out of bizarre medical mishaps. "Ooh, and one time I used it on Gladys when a human cast a revenge spell that turned her blind. It restored her sight but caused temporary insanity and a loss of bowel control for a week."

So...anal leakage *was* a concern.

Hawkyn stared at his half-brother. "Where the fuck did you get your medical training? Hogwarts?"

"Ha. Funny. I did a year and a half stint at Underworld General."

"Did they fire you, by chance?"

Darien looked hurt. "Fired is a strong word. Look, if you just...oops."

"*Oops?*" Hawk looked down at where a drop of Darien's magical mystery juice had fallen into his wound. A foul stench and hissing noise rose up as the liquid absorbed, disappearing into the mangled flesh. "Are you kidding me?"

"It was just a drop. Probably wasn't enough to affect anything," Darien said quickly. "Probably."

Hawk shoved the guy away and staggered to his feet. "Never mind. I'll just drop by the hospital."

"They treat demons," Darien reminded him. "Not angels."

He reached for the door, wincing at the stretch of his muscles. "We're half demon."

"We're half *fallen angel*," Darien argued. "There's a difference."

Not according to a lot of folks. "Have you even *met* our father? Azagoth is a demon if I ever saw one. He stopped being any kind of angel a long time ago."

Darien nodded emphatically, his long bangs flapping against his cheeks. "Especially lately."

"No shit." Hawkyn paused with the door half open. "What's up with his grumpy ass?"

Shrugging, Darien popped the rubber stopper back into the elixir bottle. "I overheard Zhubaal and Hades talking the other day. They said he's been demanding access to the Memitim Council. And several of our brothers and sisters mentioned that he's been asking them weird questions."

Hawkyn frowned. "Questions? Like what?"

"Personal stuff. It's bizarre. He's never taken an interest in us before, and now he's wanting the history of our lives."

That *was* bizarre. Azagoth had always taken a cool, detached approach to fatherhood, treating all his children more like tenants than family.

"And yesterday," Darien continued, "he was in a rage all day. Not even Lilliana dared to cross him. You should have seen him at dinner. He devoured a steak like it was someone's soul. He was fucking *snarling*."

"Yeah? You know what else is snarling?" Hawk looked down at his destroyed abdomen. "My wound, thanks to the radioactive sludge you dripped into it."

Darien laughed. "You think Underworld General will be any better?"

"Can't be worse."

Funny, but Darien had nothing to say about that, and Hawkyn wasn't sure if that was a good thing or not.

* * * *

The staff at Underworld General Hospital weren't the nicest people Hawkyn had ever met, but they fixed him quickly, and without using crazy mystery potions. They'd even called in the head doctor after Hawkyn's full sister, Idess, had explained who he was. UGH might specialize in demon care, but the children of Azagoth and siblings of Idess got first class treatment.

As he started to leave the building, located beneath the busy streets of Manhattan, Idess gave him a hug. "I'll be bringing Mace to see his grandpa tomorrow. Will you be there?"

Idess was mated to one of the Seminus brothers who ran the hospital, and they had a rambunctious, dark-haired toddler who was full of mischief and who might be just the thing to lighten Azagoth's mood.

"If I am, I'll make sure to see you guys."

She gestured to the sliding ER doors to the parking lot. "Where are you off to?"

He hesitated. Idess had broken Memitim rules for one of her Primori, so he could probably trust her, but...

"I haven't decided yet," he lied. He hesitated again, and then, well, fuck it. "Idess?"

"Yes?"

"When you were Memitim, you had to protect some real scumbags, didn't you? Including an assassin?"

She cocked an eyebrow. "Careful, little brother." Her tone, issuing a playful warning, reminded him of Suzanne. But given that he, Suzanne, and Idess were full siblings—centuries apart—he wasn't surprised. "That assassin is now my mate."

"But he's not an assassin anymore," he pointed out. "He's a partner at the hospital, and he works here, right?"

She nodded. "In the morgue."

Since the dude's bare-handed touch was fatal, working with dead people seemed like a good job for him.

"Okay," he said, "but what was it like having to protect someone who killed for money?"

"What's this about, Hawk?" Idess crossed her arms across the black scrub top she wore over a pair of jeans. She had the mom-thing down pat. "Is one of your Primori an assassin?"

"Serial killer."

She winced. "Yes, that's tough. I know that bad people affect change in human society in ways we can't understand at the time, but it's still hard to stand by and let them wreak havoc. I had to watch over a number of truly disgusting Primori in my two thousand years of service, and the ones who tortured and killed for pleasure were some of the worst."

Agreed. But somehow Hawkyn had managed to disconnect himself from his Primoris' lives, duty-bound to protect them no matter what. And he still would. But he couldn't get Aurora's eyes, wide with terror, out of his mind.

"How did you deal with it?" he asked, lowering his voice as if the hospital was full of Memitim Council members instead of vampires, demons, and werewolves. "Were you ever tempted to save the victims?"

"All the time," she sighed. "If not for my brother reining me in, I might have."

"Would that have been so bad?"

She blinked in surprise, and he couldn't blame her. He was just as surprised that those words had come out of his mouth.

"Hawkyn, I'd think you of all people would understand the need to not interfere in the lives of our Primori. Don't you want to join the Memitim Council when you Ascend? It won't happen if you break a rule like that."

Well aware of that fact, he swallowed dryly. "I'm just curious."

She didn't appear to buy it. "Once," she said, lowering her voice the way he had, "when I had a breakdown over the death of a teen girl at the hands of one of my Primori, a king who got off on raping and murdering his own subjects, a Council member broke with protocol by telling me that the king wasn't Primori because he was a great ruler who would make a difference in the world. In fact, his name has been, deservedly, lost to history. He was Primori because he was destined to kill the girl. If he hadn't, she would have given birth to someone who would have changed the course of history and made Caligula seem tame and sweet." She inhaled a ragged breath. "It's still hard to think about, but you have to trust that the system works, and remember that ninety percent of the people you protect are good. We just tend to obsess over the bad ones."

He did trust the system. But when he'd flashed into that parking lot and saw that his Primori was about to abduct a woman, Hawkyn had instinctively tried to prevent it. Now he was left with one burning question: Was Ms. Mercer fated to die at Drayger's hands...or had Hawkyn's presence prevented the escape she'd been meant to make?

Hell, maybe *Drayger's* fate had been to die from the blast that Hawkyn had taken instead. If so, Hawk's interference had changed history. And, if so, he was in a *lot* of trouble. He could kiss membership in the Memitim Council goodbye... And that was assuming he was even allowed to Ascend and become a true angel in the first place.

"Thanks, Idess," he mumbled.

"You're welcome. I'll see you later." She narrowed her eyes, going all big sister on him. "And don't do anything stupid."

"Wouldn't dream of it."

Except that was a lie. He had to find Aurora before Drayger killed her, and he could only pray that he'd taken her to one of the places Hawk knew about. The guy seemed to have an unusual number of dungeons, and according to Drayger's previous Memitim guardian, he moved his victims around, rarely keeping them in one place for more than a couple of days. If he held true to his pattern, Aurora would be kept alive for two weeks in three different locations.

Hawk just had to hope Drayger didn't deviate from his usual routine as he'd done a couple of times in the past.

Cursing softly, Hawkyn stepped out into the underground parking lot, which wasn't protected by Underworld General's ward preventing entry and exit via any means but the ER doors and the Harrowgate. Once outside, he squared his shoulders and released his wings, shadowy appendages that made him unique amongst his wingless siblings and which allowed him to cloak himself in a bubble of invisibility.

His brothers and sisters could also make themselves invisible, but they didn't look as cool doing it.

Wings fully extended and invisibility cloak engaged, he brushed his fingers over Drayger's mark on his wrist and was instantly transported to his Primori's location, an office building in downtown Portland.

Drayger was at Interim, a computer software company where he worked as a database developer. It was both good news and bad that he was here. It meant he wasn't harming anyone, but it also meant that Aurora would be harder to find.

The human looked so non-threatening sitting at his desk in khakis and a green company polo, his *I <3 Computers* mug filled with steaming coffee, knickknacks and a photo of his mom nearby. All an attempt to appear normal. Psychopaths were often surprisingly adept at fitting in. Drayger was a chameleon, and he was good at it.

But Hawkyn had seen the real Drayger. He'd seen what was under the face Drayger wore in public and when he was playing with his victims. The true man beneath the mask still appeared human, but the humanity was gone. His eyes were cold and dead, his posture erect with the kind of deranged confidence that only those who didn't fear pain or death possessed. A dark energy surrounded him, the seductive kind that drew other evil beings.

And he could turn it on and off in a heartbeat.

Hawkyn despised the bastard, was sickened that someone like him rated angelic protection. But Hawk would be first in line to kill the fucker once the protection was no longer needed. Angels were forbidden to kill humans no matter how evil they were, but every once in a while permission to do so was granted, and Hawkyn intended to secure authorization to rid the planet of one Jason Drayger no matter the cost.

Satisfied that Drayger was occupied, Hawk flashed to the first of several hideouts, an old cellar at an abandoned country farmhouse. It was empty of everything but a filthy mattress, bloodstains, and nasty tools he used for his gruesome hobby.

Same results in Drayger's residence, the shed on the property Drayger cared for while his brother, Ben, was overseas doing contract work for an oil company, and the cave hidden deep in the Mt. Hood National Forest.

The weird thing about the cave was the lack of obvious torture tools and a mattress. Only a hammer, a rusty hand saw, a hatchet, and a few ropes lay in neat coils on the cave floor, nothing that would be suspicious for anyone stumbling upon the place.

Well, shit. Those spots were the only ones Hawkyn knew about.

Where was she? What had Drayger done to her already? And what was Hawkyn going to do once he found her?

Maybe there was a way to find out if his Primori's fate was still on track...which would mean that Hawkyn hadn't screwed up. But it would also mean that Aurora Mercer was exactly where she was supposed to be.

And while that would be good news for Hawkyn's future, it would be very, very bad for hers.

Chapter Four

Hawkyn's gut was churning as he paced back and forth at the Summoning Stone, a football-sized rose quartz placed in the center of a newly-built gazebo at the edge of the Memitim training center in Sheoul-gra. With any luck, someone from the Memitim embassy in Heaven would pop down here to see him, but in his experience, there only seemed to be a 50/50 chance of that happening...which was still far better odds than getting someone from the Memitim Council to show up. If they had ever visited Sheoul-gra, he wasn't aware of it.

He'd give the embassy fifteen more minutes, and then he was out of here.

Footsteps behind him had him spinning around in relief, but when he saw his father standing there in black slacks and a button-down shirt, intense green eyes blazing like hot emeralds, Hawkyn's gut dropped to his booted feet.

"Hawkyn." Azagoth's deep voice sent a shimmer of dread through Hawk's very marrow. His father was intimidating on the best of days, but lately his mood had been as black as his hair and clothes.

Steeling himself, Hawkyn inclined his head in greeting. "Yes, sir."

"I heard you were injured."

"I was, but I'm fine now." He gestured in the direction of the armory, where he was in charge of inventory and acquisitions. "If you're wondering about that report you asked for, I sent it to your desk yesterday—"

Azagoth waved his hand. "I'll get to it this afternoon." He stared at Hawkyn long enough to make him begin to sweat, and just as Hawk started to fidget, his father spoke. "You've never told me about your childhood."

Hawk swallowed, remembering that Darien had told him Azagoth had been asking weird personal questions. "No, sir, I haven't."

"Tell me."

"I really don't think it's important—"

The breeze turned chilly, mirroring Azagoth's voice, and Hawkyn resisted the urge to shiver. "Would I ask if it wasn't important?"

Hawkyn ignored the rhetorical question. "My childhood was no different than any other Memitim's." Except Suzanne, who had led a charmed existence before her first Memitim mentor had plucked her from her human life. "It sucked." At Azagoth's cocked eyebrow, Hawkyn knew he wasn't going to get away with a vague explanation. His father wanted details, and only a moron denied Azagoth what he wanted. "I grew up in a workhouse in London. The people who ran it said I was left on the doorstep as a newborn."

"No one adopted you?"

He laughed. "Children who were 'adopted' back then were often taken to be used as slaves or apprentices."

"Children who lived in the workhouses and orphanages weren't treated any better, no?"

Not really, no. And why the hell were they talking about this? Reluctantly, he answered his father's question before he became impatient. An impatient Azagoth was a scary Azagoth.

Then again, so was a patient Azagoth.

"As soon as we were able, we were forced to pay for our care. We got money however we could. Begging, stealing, doing odd jobs, prostitution."

Azagoth's expression didn't change, and yet Hawk could feel the anger billowing off him. But why? As far as Hawk knew, Azagoth didn't give a shit about how his children had grown up. He'd always said that *now* was what mattered. They'd grown up the way they had in order to shape them into warriors. It had all been for the greater good and all that standard issue bullshit.

"Was there ever a time when it wasn't bad? When you were happy?"

Happy? Was Azagoth fucking kidding?

The memories he'd thought were long buried came rushing back at him, and with it, the anger. The feelings of abandonment. Back then he'd thought he was human and that his human parents, probably devastatingly poor, had given him up as a last resort.

Now, knowing his parents were powerful beyond imagining and had intentionally left him in a shitty situation, he was even angrier. Yes, he knew why they'd done it. And he'd always been able to conceal his emotions. But he could no longer deny that those emotions, that fury and hurt, had been seething just below the surface of his mind for centuries.

"No, Father, it was always bad." Hawk's hands curled into fists at his sides. "I don't remember ever having a full belly or being clean. I was never happy. Not once. Not ever. Not until the day my Memitim mentor arrived to rescue me from the hell that was my life. He might even have saved my life. I was about to lose a hand for stealing a crust of bread."

For a long time, Azagoth said nothing. He merely stood there, his eyes glinting like green glass as he stared at Hawkyn.

Finally, he gestured over Hawkyn's shoulder. "You have company."

Hawk wheeled around to find Jacob, a Memitim who had Ascended nearly a century ago, standing near the Summoning Stone. His mink brown wings that matched his hair and eyes were fully extended, probably to show them off to his lowly, un-Ascended half-brother.

"What do you want?" he asked in a snooty tone.

"I—" Hawkyn turned to Azagoth, but their father had disappeared. Well, that was one less thing to worry about.

"You what?"

Damn, but Jacob was annoying. But then, he'd been annoying even before he'd been given his wings and a cushy job at the Memitim embassy, which was really more of a regulatory agency, but whatever.

"I know we aren't supposed to be privy to our Primoris' futures, but would we know if their futures have gone off track?"

Jacob adjusted the crimson sash that kept his embassy-issued metallic silver and bronze robes closed. "Why are you asking?"

"I dunno," Hawkyn said casually. "I'm just curious."

"I see." Jacob put away his wings in a whoosh of air that ruffled Hawkyn's hair. "You wouldn't know. We would."

Hawkyn's breath backed up in his lungs like cement, and he couldn't move any air for half a dozen thudding heartbeats. Had Drayger's fate line gone off track, and did the embassy assholes know?

Stay calm. "How?"

Jacob studied his nails, dragging this out, clearly enjoying the power he wielded. The weasel.

Finally, he folded his arms across his chest, making his robes swing around his bare feet. "Every Primori has a file of sorts," he explained. "These files are monitored, and if anything goes awry or the Primori dies before his time, we get an alert."

"What happens after you get an alert?"

Jacob huffed as if irritated with the conversation. "It varies. Sometimes we let the situation sort itself out. Sometimes we warn the Primori's Memitim guardian that they'd better rectify the situation, and sometimes there's nothing we can do but try to mitigate the damage by rearranging the lives of others to get the results we need." He paused, locking gazes with Hawk. "Is there anything you want to tell me?"

"Not at all." Hawkyn smiled, hoping Jacob bought his bullshit. "I'm just hoping to join the Memitim Council one day, so I'm trying to learn all the behind-the-scenes stuff now."

Jacob laughed. "You think that'll give you an edge? Idiot. I've been a full angel for decades now, and I'm not even on the waiting list to merely *apply* to join the Council."

"Maybe you should have been asking questions before you Ascended," Hawkyn offered. "Like I am." Jacob had always been a slacker, doing the bare minimum of work needed to get the job done.

"Fuck you." Baring his teeth, Jacob flared his wings again. "I spoke with your mother the other day. Did you know she's on the Council? She joined recently. Introduced me to her mate and three beautiful children. Most of our mothers never had families because of the guilt they feel for giving us up. But not yours. She dotes on her children. Loves them like crazy." His smile turned malevolent. "Have you ever even met her? Where did she leave you as a baby, I wonder..."

Hawkyn decked the asshole. Just slammed his fist into Jacob's perfect face. The crunch of bone was the most satisfying thing Hawkyn had felt in years. Didn't matter that Jacob's bones mended in an instant and that the blood vanished without a trace. It felt good.

"You," Jacob snarled, "are lucky I have someplace to be right now. But watch your back, little brother."

Jacob flashed out of Sheoul-gra before Hawkyn could respond. Lucky for Jacob, since Hawk's response would have been a lot more painful than a punch in the face.

Chapter Five

Within seconds of Jacob flashing out of Sheoul-gra, Hawkyn did the same. Then he spent nearly every minute of the next thirty-six hours shadowing Jason Drayger...with nothing to show for it.

Hawkyn had left Drayger alone only twice. The first time was during a four-hour period when one of his other five Primori was in danger—danger that never materialized. But when Hawk returned to Drayger, the guy had been driving home, blood spattered on his shirt and pants.

It had been Aurora's blood, and Hawk knew it. He'd felt sick to his stomach and furious that he'd missed an opportunity to locate her. Guilt had weighed him down like a wet shroud, and out of guilt, he'd left Drayger to shower and go to bed, and Hawk had gone to Aurora's house to see who she was.

To see who Drayger was hurting.

As Hawkyn had wandered through her little one-bedroom house in Portland's quirky Pearl District, he couldn't help but smile at her cheery '50s retro decor and the delicate spun glass and stained glass ornaments hanging in her windows. Hedgehog figurines and scented candles lined a couple of small shelves, and, while she had a few framed family photos on the walls, there were far more artsy pictures of Portland and the surrounding area.

Her place was cozy and warm, and he got the impression that this was more than a home for Aurora; it was a sanctuary. From her overstuffed furniture to the yoga mat in the corner, the gurgling water fountain in the entryway, and the Japanese rock garden that filled her tiny outdoor space out back, her house was a soothing retreat.

Which made sense when he discovered that she was a masseuse at an exclusive nearby spa.

Every discovery Hawkyn made only strengthened his resolve to help her. He just needed to find her first.

Hopefully, that was going to happen now.

Drayger was on the move again. This was it. Hawk knew it.

You can't interfere.

No, technically he couldn't. But he had to do *something*. Aurora's magic had been wasted on Hawk when she could have used it on Drayger. What if she was supposed to have gotten away? What if his interference had caused her capture? By saving her he'd be righting a wrong. Setting Drayger's future back on course. Maybe. Hopefully.

Sounded good to him.

Shadow wings out and the *shrowd* engaged, Hawkyn sat in the backseat of Drayger's unassuming beige Ford Escort and listened to the too-loud, incoherent screech of some heavy metal band as they navigated the streets of one of Portland's industrial areas. Drayger had picked up some cheap fast-food burgers and had eaten one, but the others sat next to him in a bag, the greasy stench filling the interior. Finally, Drayger pulled into a junkyard, unlocked the gate, and parked the car near a shipping crate tucked in a rear corner of the lot.

Hawkyn's pulse quickened with anticipation as Drayger opened the creaky door and stepped inside.

And there, huddled in a corner on a filthy mattress, was Aurora, her long blond hair tangled and matted. She reminded Hawkyn of a chained, neglected animal, and his hands clenched in fists of hot rage. She was naked except for panties and a ratty, stained AC/DC T-shirt Drayger must have given her, and her exposed skin was bruised and crusted with dried blood. Her bloodshot eyes were bright with fear, but also defiance. Hawk had seen that look so many times over the centuries, from soldiers who knew they were cornered by the enemy but were determined to go down fighting, to abused women who had had enough.

Fierce respect swelled inside Hawkyn's chest, and he found himself torn between wanting to comfort her and wanting to fight beside her.

"Hope you're hungry today," Drayger said as he held up the bag of food.

"Fuck you," she rasped, and Hawkyn couldn't help but admire her spirit. "I'm not playing the puke game with you again."

"You either eat the food so I can watch you throw it up from the pain, or I gut punch you until you throw up bile. Your choice. Personally, I think it's better to be able to puke something up, but whatever. Dry heaves are a choice, I guess."

Hawk's own stomach turned over. How could he have forgotten that Drayger loved to watch his victims vomit while being tortured?

You know how.

Yes, he did. Like most of his brethren, he was capable of compartmentalizing, separating his feelings from his job and locking the bad shit in a virtual box that rarely had to be opened. Because opening that box could wreck even the most callous of warriors and destroy the vital objectivity and distance required to do one's duty.

Aurora closed her eyes and shuddered. "Why are you doing this?"

"Because I have to," Drayger said, his tone chillingly ho-hum. "I'm sure there's some underlying pathology, some traumatic break I endured as a child, but what it comes down to is that I get off on causing fear and pain."

She opened her eyes, the dim light making the exhausted circles around them even darker. "That doesn't mean you have to."

"Wrong." Drayger inhaled as if savoring the scent of her misery, the fucker. "Imagine having nothing to live for. Imagine a depression so deep you can't climb out of it. I'm dead inside. Nothing makes me happy. Nothing makes me feel. Nothing except what I do to women like you. Knowing I'm ridding the earth of magic-using scum gives me a reason to live." He dropped the bag of food on the floor and reached for a scalpel on his tray of torture instruments. "So let's get started."

Shit. Hawk had to stop him, but how? He couldn't very well pop out of thin air and trash the guy. Of all Memitim rules, harming your own Primori was the biggest no-no. An offense so egregious that one could, potentially, lose their freedom...or their life.

Which meant that Hawkyn had to lure Jason away.

Or *scare* him away.

Quickly, Hawkyn zapped himself outside and searched for a suitable projectile. As he picked up a rusty crowbar, a bloodcurdling scream, muffled by the metal walls, filled him with even greater urgency. And rage.

Imagining that Drayger was sitting in his vehicle's passenger seat, Hawkyn hurled the metal rod through the passenger side window. Glass sprayed into the air, but it would have been far more satisfying if the shards had been made of Drayger's skull. The car alarm blared, drowning out the tinkle of glass pelting the ground.

Still invisible, he flashed back into the cargo container just as Drayger heaved open the door and peered outside. Inside, Aurora dangled helplessly from chains, blood dripping from one partially skinned thigh, and it took every ounce of control Hawkyn could muster to keep from releasing her right then and there.

Mercifully, she'd passed out, but the fact that she couldn't, at this moment, feel pain didn't make Hawkyn feel any better. If anything, his anger level went up a notch, making him tremble with the desire to slaughter Drayger the way he would have if the guy hadn't been Primori. Damn the rules. Damn this job. Hawk hated it. He was good at it, but son of a bitch, he despised it sometimes.

The day Hawkyn swore in as a Council member, shit was gonna change.

Drayger scanned the deepening twilight before he ventured out to turn off his car alarm. Looking as nervous as Hawk had ever seen him, the bastard scurried back to the container, frowned at Aurora as she hung limply from the chains, and slammed the sliding door closed.

Hawkyn flashed out long enough to watch Drayger take off, and then he went back inside and lowered the female's unconscious body to the metal floor. The anger inside him raged even harder as he gathered her petite frame in his arms. She needed medical attention, but he couldn't take her to a human hospital. There would be too many questions, police, and eventually her statements would lead to Drayger's arrest.

So what?

The question flashed in his thoughts a dozen times before logic and duty brought him back to reality. Like it or not, the scumbag was vital to humanity in some way, and Hawkyn had a duty to make sure Drayger fulfilled his destiny. Besides, maybe by removing Aurora from the equation he could set things right.

Maybe.

Please let this set things right.

Holding her securely and trying not to think about how cold and fragile she felt, he flashed himself to UGH's underground parking lot and strode through the sliding Emergency Department doors for the second time in as many days. Instantly, a hairy male nurse with a snout and a female nurse with tiny horns jutting from her temples jogged over and directed him to a cubicle, where he laid Aurora on a waiting wheeled exam table.

A female in a white lab coat embroidered with a modified caduceus and the name "Blaspheme, MD" joined him and asked questions as the other two prepared IVs and performed checks of Aurora's vitals.

"What species is she?" Blaspheme asked.

"I'm not sure," Hawkyn said, "but I'm guessing she's at least half human."

She nodded and gestured to the male nurse. "Run a DNA DB test, STAT."

"DNA DB?" Hawk stepped aside so the nurse could slip past.

"DNA Database," she said as she cut through Aurora's T-shirt. "We can run her DNA against all the logged species in our database to see if we can find a match."

"If not?"

"Then she'll be listed as a new unknown species until she regains consciousness and tells us." She barked some orders laden with strange medical terms at the remaining nurse and then turned back to Hawkyn. "What happened to her, and how are you involved?"

He blinked at the forcefulness of the question, and when he caught the nurse staring at him it occurred to him that this could easily appear to be a case of domestic violence. It kind of surprised him that demons would give a crap about such things.

"She was imprisoned and tortured by a serial killer. I rescued her." He could have explained in more detail, but he figured it was probably best to keep the fact that he was an angel under wraps in a demon hospital. Yes, he'd had to reveal his identity when he was treated yesterday, and several staff members knew he was Idess's brother, but she'd assured him that no one would blab. Apparently, the doctor who ran the hospital was a stickler for rules.

As if Aurora knew she was being discussed, she moaned. Her eyes flickered open and locked with his, swirling with fear and confusion that he actually felt. Understood. Because hundreds of years ago at the age of eighteen, he'd been beaten, tortured, and caged while waiting for his turn at the chopping block. The only question was whether he'd lose one hand or two for stealing the bread he'd been desperately hungry for.

Then he'd woken in a soft bed in a castle in Belgium, surrounded by strangers and confused as hell. So he knew what Aurora was experiencing, and instinctively, he reached for her hand.

Blaspheme blocked him, and in that instant, he realized she was no demon. Her energy, dancing on his skin like butterfly wings, was angelic.

Blaspheme was an angel. Her heavenly vibe was weak, so she wasn't a full-fledged Heavenly resident, but neither did she emit the shadowy vibe of an Unfallen, the evil vibe of a True Fallen, or the flat, stale vibe of a fellow Memitim. Interesting.

"I need you to hang out in the waiting room," she said sternly, leaving no room for argument. "Or you can leave your contact information and I'll update you when I can."

As reluctant as he was to leave Aurora, he understood duty.

And it was a good thing, too, because if he didn't, Drayger would be dead by now.

* * * *

Scalpels and bone saws. Grotesque scenes of gore and body parts. Bits of flesh and hair sticking to tarps. A handsome man reaching for her but unable to connect. Snarling monsters emerging from the fog in dark parking lots. The rattle of chains, the stench of burning blood. The man was reaching for her again, but she was being dragged away by clawed hands. No!

Aurora woke to the sounds of screams. It was only after a warm hand closed over hers that she opened her eyes and realized that the screams had come from her. As her blurry vision cleared, chains on the ceiling came into sharp focus, and another scream lodged in her throat.

There are chains on the ceiling.

She lurched upright in bed, her heart pounding, her breaths coming in spastic gasps. Where was she? And who was the hot blond guy dressed in jeans and leather sitting next to her bed? He looked familiar...especially those piercing emerald eyes.

There are chains on the fucking ceiling!

A vision of him in a dark parking lot flashed in her mind, and she saw herself blasting him in the chest with every drop of power she'd been able to muster.

He was the man reaching for her over and over.

He was real.

Oh, God, the nightmares had been real. Not dreams, but memories.

Her throat closed up even as her lungs tried to take in air. Everything closed in on her, turning her own body into a prison. Or a coffin. Was this what claustrophobia felt like? She wanted to scream, to flail, but where would that get her?

Close your eyes. Calm down. Focus on breathing. It was what she told her tense clients at the spa. Breathe. In. Out. In. Out.

Open your eyes. Feel the peace.

There were still chains on the ceiling.

"Hey, it's okay." The man covered her cold hand with his warm one. "You're safe now." The stranger's deep voice soothed her, which made no sense, given that he was part of her nightmare.

You whacked some Good Samaritan who was probably trying to help you.

Okay, yes, Drayger the Psychopath had claimed this guy was innocent, a potential rescuer. But Jason Drayger was also a twisted monster who couldn't be trusted.

She yanked her hand away. "Who are you? Where am I?" Her voice was hoarse, her throat tender from screaming.

"You're at Underworld General Hospital. And I'm Hawkyn."

Which told her nothing. And... Had he said *Underworld* General Hospital?

The door to the room swung open, and a woman in Spongebob Squarepants scrubs and a lab coat entered.

"Good morning," she said cheerily, her fuchsia-tipped brunette pigtails bobbing as she walked. "I'm Doctor Gemella Morgan, but you can call me Gem." Another female followed her inside, a red-skinned demon female with tiny black horns, her whip-like tail swishing against her legs as she walked. Holy shit.

Holy. Shit.

Gem glanced at Hawkyn. "Could you give us some privacy?"

He inclined his head and shoved to his feet, his black leather jacket creaking as he stood. For some reason, Aurora didn't like the idea of him leaving. Maybe because, right now, he was the only thing familiar about any of this, even if their history only went back as far as a dark parking lot.

"Aurora," he said in his whiskey-smooth voice, "I have some other people to check on, but I'll be back soon."

She nodded numbly, unsure how to respond. He was a complete stranger. Why would he care about her enough to come back?

She watched him saunter out of the room, not ashamed in the least to admire the way his butt looked in his worn jeans. He might be a stranger, but he was a well put together one. And hey, her ancestors were sex demons, so admiring male assets was in her nature.

And his assets were spectacular.

As soon as he was gone, the demon put down a tray of food on the counter and followed him out, leaving her with the doctor.

Gem put her fingers to Aurora's wrist. "How are you feeling?" she asked in a humdrum voice as if this was all perfectly normal.

Aurora had encountered demons before, but few of those encounters had been pleasant. Seeing them working in a setting as normal as a hospital, even if it was a bizarre one with black floors, ceiling chains, and skulls on shelves, left her at a loss for coherent thought.

"I'm feeling like I'm in the Twilight Zone," she rasped. "Am I really in an underworld hospital?"

Gem pointed to the stylized caduceus on her jacket and the "Underworld General Hospital" script beneath it. "Yep. We specialize in pain."

That sounded a bit ominous. "Relieving it...or giving it?"

"That," Gem said with a waggle of eyebrows, "depends on the circumstances." She gestured to the sheet covering Aurora's legs. "Mind if I take a look? The doctor who treated you when you first arrived used a new salve to regrow your skin and I want to see how it's coming along. It only works on people who have at least some human in their DNA, and it doesn't work on all demon/human combinations, so we aren't sure how complete the heal will be for you."

"Ah...okay," Aurora said, having no other real options.

Gem smiled reassuringly. "You can trust me. I'm a doctor."

"Are you a demon?" That Aurora was asking a *doctor* if she was a demon added another layer to the Twilight Zone sensation.

Gem folded back the sheet to expose Aurora's legs. "Yes, ma'am. But I'm also half human, so I promise I won't eat you." Aurora stared, unsure if Gem was being serious or not, and Gem laughed. "That was a joke. I don't eat humans. No one at this hospital does." She paused, looking thoughtful. "Well, the vampires do, I guess. And sometimes the werewolves have an accident. But not inside the hospital," she added quickly. "We're under an anti-violence ward."

Relieved that she wasn't about to be eaten, Aurora sank back into her pillow. "This is so bizarre," she whispered, mainly to herself, but Gem laughed.

"You act as if you aren't at least part demon." Gem looked up. "I'm guessing you were raised in the human realm?" At Aurora's nod, Gem continued. "We weren't able to determine your species or identify whether or not you're a human/demon crossbreed. Can you help out with that?"

This was so crazy. But these people seemed like they were trying to help, and Aurora didn't see any reason to lie about her species. "We call ourselves Wytches."

"Like human witches?"

"With a 'Y'."

"I see." The doctor probed Aurora's wound with her fingers, but it didn't hurt at all. "What makes you different from witches with an 'I'?"

"For one thing, we aren't entirely human." For another, their abilities were part of them, activated by thoughts or single commands rather than spell books, chants, potions, or charmed objects.

Gem gave her a quizzical look. "Do you know your origins?"

For some sketchy superstitious reasons, Aurora's people rarely spoke about their ancient history, preferring to concentrate on their history since the rebellion that had gained them freedom and life among humans. Aurora had always thought the reluctance to discuss their origins was ridiculous, but then, she'd long ago adopted a human lifestyle and left behind Wytch lore, customs and, especially, mating rituals.

"According to lore," she said, trying to sound like she wasn't mentally rolling her eyes, "we were created when a Charnel Apostle sorcerer mated male human witches with a breed of succubus that's now extinct."

"Huh." One of Gem's dark eyebrows climbed up her forehead. "So what kinds of abilities do you possess?"

Startled by a question Wytches considered rude, Aurora stiffened. "I'm sorry, but I'd like to keep that information to myself."

Gem smiled, apparently not offended by Aurora's sharp tone. "That's your right, and I absolutely understand. Now, let's take a closer look at this leg."

The doctor approved of the way the wound was healing, but all Aurora could do when she looked at the mess on her thigh was remember the pain of the knife and orgasmic gleam in Drayger's eyes as she bled and screamed.

"Hey," Gem said softly, and Aurora realized she was trembling. "It's okay. You're safe here. No one will hurt you. I promise." She took Aurora's hand and gave it a comforting squeeze, but her fingers weren't near the spot on Aurora's palm that would allow her to absorb the doctor's energy. If she could shift just a little to the left, she could replenish her powers... "We took care of the injuries we could see, but did your captor hurt you...in other ways?"

Rape. She was talking about rape. Forgetting the need to steal a little of Gem's magic-giving energy, Aurora shuddered.

"No. He cut off my clothes, but...no."

The memory of it, the fear as he stripped her, brought a wave of fresh anxiety. He'd led her to believe he was going to sexually assault her, but his taunts turned out to be just another way to terrorize her. In the end, he was too disgusted by what she was to be turned on.

"Good," Gem said crisply. "And I hope he's too dead to hurt anyone else."

Ditto. *Big* ditto. "Who...who brought me here?"

"Hawkyn." The doctor released her and reached for a box of bandages. "He's the one who rescued you."

"Why? How did he find me? How did he survive what I did to him?"

Gem eyed her. "What did you do to him?" She shook her head, making her perky pigtails swing around her jawline. "You know what? Never mind. All I know is that he brought you in and demanded the best medical team available." She let out a sigh as she loosely covered the wound with a fresh gauze pad. "Typical angel."

It took a second for Aurora to process Gem's words, but even then, they didn't make sense. "Did...did you say he's an *angel*?"

"Oh, shit." Swearing again, Gem settled the sheet and blanket over Aurora's legs. "I thought you knew. He's sort of an angel... I'll let him fill you in on the details since I wasn't supposed to say anything in the first place." She glanced at her watch. "I've got an appointment, but I'll have a nurse come clean your wound and apply another coat of salve. You should be able to go home tonight, and you'll be fully healed by morning." She brought the tray of food over and settled it on the bed's table attachment. "Want me to send Hawkyn back in?"

Aurora's breath caught. She associated him with the worst few days of her life, but at the same time, it appeared that she owed him that same life. Plus, she'd hurt him that night when he was, according to Drayger, trying to help her.

"Please," she told Gem. "I have a lot of questions for him."

"I'm sure you do." Gem reached for the door handle. "I don't know him well, but his sister is part of my family, so for what it's worth, I think you can trust him."

"Thank you, Doctor."

Nodding, Gem left. Before the door whispered closed, Hawkyn caught it, stepped inside, and the air rushed out of Aurora's lungs. But this time, her physical response wasn't the result of trauma or fear. This time it was pure female appreciation. And maybe a bit of awe that the tall, devastatingly handsome male was an angel. An actual angel.

Gods, she had so many questions.

"Hi," he said, flashing a smile that would have dropped her panties in any other situation. Not even the fangs that peeked between his full lips would have given her pause. Except, maybe, to ask why an angel would have fangs. "How are you feeling?"

"I'm not in pain, if that's what you mean." She opened the little bottle of orange juice and took a sip. "The doctor said you're an angel. Was she joking?" Because angels didn't wear ass-hugging jeans and untucked blue plaid button-downs, right? They wore robes and sandals or something.

"She wasn't joking."

Oh, wow. She exhaled slowly, needing a little time to gather her thoughts. Why would an angel have been in the parking lot that night, and why would he rescue her? Unless... "Are you my guardian angel?"

He moved closer, his boots silent on the gleaming black floor. "Long story, but no." He looked down, his long bangs falling across his face and obscuring his eyes. "I'm sorry I couldn't save you from him." He didn't have to say who "him" was. "I failed."

"Are you kidding me? I blasted you with silver fire. I thought you were with that bastard who abducted me." The sound of his body hitting the lamp post reverberated in her ears as if it had happened only seconds ago. "Later, when he said you were a Good Samaritan, I was afraid I'd killed you."

His hand came up to rub his sternum. "You put a serious hurting on me, but we angels are pretty tough."

Apparently so. A Wytch's silver fire weapon was so deadly they were forbidden to use it except to save their own life. She'd never heard of anyone surviving a full-body strike. But then, she'd never heard of it being used against an angel.

"How did you find me?" She frowned. "*Why* did you find me?"

He shoved his hand through his sandy hair, and bizarrely, she wondered what it felt like. Was it as silky as it looked? Did angels have perfect, super-soft hair? What about their wings? Would it be rude to ask?

"Another long story," he sighed. "I just wish I'd found you sooner."

Yeah, she wished that, too, but she wasn't going to complain that he hadn't saved her life sooner. That he'd saved it at all was a miracle.

"Please tell me he's dead." She'd never wished death on anyone, but Drayger needed to die slowly and in excruciating pain.

"I would love to tell you that," Hawkyn said, his voice dripping with raw anger. "But I won't let him hurt you again."

Footsteps passed by the door, reminding her how weird this whole thing was. "Excuse me, but... You're an angel. You brought me to a hospital full of demons? Aren't angels and demons mortal enemies?" Hell, she should be his enemy as well.

"Well..."

She held up a hand to stop him. "Are you going to tell me it's another long story?"

The red tinge in his cheeks said yes. "Let's just say it's complicated."

"I'm sure it is." She peeled the top slice of bread from the sandwich on her tray. Looked like ham and cheese. She liked ham. But then, this was a demon hospital... Maybe it *wasn't* ham. Ew. Appetite ruined, she pushed the tray away. "What is the angelic stance on Wytches?"

"We have no problem with witches."

"Just to be clear, it's Wytch. With a Y."

His eyes shot wide. "Seriously? I've never met one. I always thought you were mythical." He shrugged, a slow roll of one big shoulder. She'd bet those broad shoulders carried a lot of weight, and her fingers itched to knead the tension out of them. "Of course, I always thought elves were mythical too, but last year one of the fallen angels who works for my father mated one."

Elves? And who the hell was his father? She was about to ask who Hawkyn's father was and why a fallen angel would be working for him when the door opened and a pretty, dark-skinned nurse entered. This one looked human, but somehow Aurora doubted that she was.

"Hi, Aurora," she said. "I'm Shanea, and I'm going to take care of you."

Hawkyn stood, rising to his full height, which was somewhere around six and a half feet, she guessed. "I'll give you some privacy."

Instinct made Aurora want to ask him to stay. She didn't know anything about him, but he'd been there for her in the grocery store parking lot, he'd rescued her, and he'd sat at her bedside while she recovered. Right now, he was the one thing in her life that made her feel safe.

She couldn't even call her brother because he was in some Middle East hellhole, and her parents were just two weeks into a year-long cruise around the world. No way was she going to interrupt anyone.

"Are you coming back?" Aurora asked, hoping the eagerness in her voice wasn't as obvious to Hawkyn as it was to her. "Will I see you again?"

His smile made her pulse flutter, and it even made Shanea sigh a little. "Absolutely."

He took off like a shot, disappearing before the door swung closed, leaving her with far more questions than answers.

But he also left her with something to look forward to, and that hadn't happened in a long, long time.

Chapter Six

Azagoth couldn't remember the last time he'd been nervous about anything. After all, he ruled his own realm and was one of the most powerful beings in existence.

But the thought of seeing his daughter Idess and her son, his grandchild, made him twitchy, and it had for the last few months. Ever since the day he learned the details about her past.

He hadn't been able to even look at Idess without thinking of how she'd grown up, and how desperate she was to protect her son from life's ugliness. Because that was what a parent did.

You didn't know.

No, for a long time he hadn't known how she, or any of his children grew up. Their mothers had placed them with human parents, and he didn't see them until they were fully grown, sometimes centuries later, more often never at all. A few had shared with him their experiences of life when they'd believed they were human, and their stories were horrific.

But Azagoth hadn't felt pity. Or sorrow. Or guilt. Before Lilliana, he'd been as cold as an arctic stone. His offspring were tough, and they'd survived. Their pasts had hardened them, turned them into the warriors they needed to be.

No, he hadn't cared at all about their misery.

Then Lilliana came along and shattered the layer of ice that had encased his heart. It had been incredible and life-giving, but now that he'd opened his realm to all his Memitim offspring, more and more of his children were showing up and telling him about their "human" lives. With few exceptions, just one, really, their stories were full of the kind of shit that gave people nightmares.

Idess's story in particular had been a tale of horror, slavery, and abuse that made him want to go back in time and slaughter every fucker who had messed with his baby girl.

Lilliana could make that happen. As an angel with the ability to time-travel, she could help him get bloody revenge for all his children. But doing so would mess with incalculable timelines and would earn him a death sentence from God himself. His only consolation was that a handful of the scum who had made his children's lives miserable were, in fact, imprisoned in the Inner Sanctum, where he could torture their useless souls for all eternity.

His hands actually shook as he joined Idess and Lilliana at the picnic table in the gazebo Lilliana had built near the brook that ran behind his palace. Little Mace gave him a big grin as he sat nearby playing with building blocks. Looked like he was creating a dog. Or, more likely, a hellhound.

"Father," Idess said, coming to her feet to greet him. Of all his offspring, only Idess would show him physical affection, and she did so now, giving him a brief hug and a peck on the cheek as she pulled away.

It made him shake harder. What the everfucking hell was wrong with him?

"Have a seat." Lilliana, her long chestnut hair framing her ageless face, patted the bench next to her. "We were just about to pour some wine and discuss ideas Idess had for bringing more Memitim to Sheoul-gra." Reaching for the wine bottle, she gave him a playful wink. "Idess seems to think that more of them aren't coming to live here because you're scary."

Lilliana's tone was teasing, her smile bright, but the underlying truth, that his children were afraid of him, suddenly made an impact, cratering out his chest cavity like a meteor strike. He'd never cared about that in the past. Hell, he was proud of the fact that his offspring feared him. Fear...respect... It was all the same, right?

"Am I scary, Idess?" he asked, trying to sound...not scary.

Idess thrust her wine glass out at Lilliana. "Um, yes. Absolutely."

Still standing, he glanced over at Mace, who was tasting a building block now. "And yet, you brought your child to see me."

"Just a couple of years ago, I wouldn't have," she admitted. "But things have changed." She gave Lilliana a secret smile that wasn't as secret as she probably thought it was.

"I'd like to think I played a role in that," Lilliana said, as if she didn't know that she was the sole reason he wasn't still a monster.

Because of Lilliana he had feelings. "Yeah, I'm a real boy now."

She laughed, her amber eyes sparkling as she finished pouring the wine. "Look at you, referencing Pinocchio. The movies I make you watch are paying off."

"Yeah, well, Pinocchio got turned back into a puppet."

Idess shook her head. "You're thinking of what happened to him in one of the Shrek movies."

Ah, right. He liked the Shrek films. Ogres weren't usually that funny.

Mace held out his arms and Idess scooped him up. "Do you want to hold your grandson?"

He stared at the squirming toddler, his heart racing, his mouth dry. Even his palms had begun to sweat. The child was the most innocent thing to have ever stepped foot in this realm, and Azagoth was the most evil. His hands... His hands had done things that child would never even be able to comprehend, and they didn't belong anywhere near such purity.

"I can't." He backed up a few steps, hoping he didn't look as panicked as he felt. "I'll drop him."

Lilliana stood, concern darkening her gorgeous eyes. "Darling, what's wrong?"

"Nothing," he said, still backing up. "I just have things to do. Appointments. I have to go." He didn't care that he looked like an idiot. He had to get out of there. "Idess, I'll ah... I'll see you later."

He didn't wait for a reply. He flashed into his office, his heart pounding, his breath burning in his throat.

What the fuck was happening to him?

With trembling hands, he poured himself a double shot of tequila from the bar on the far wall, downed it, and poured another. As he raised the glass to his lips for the second time, he noticed the flashing light on his communications pad.

He scanned the message from Jim Bob, one of his Heavenly spies, and trashed it. He wasn't interested in low-level gossip speculating about the mysterious author of a new comic book series that was outing a lot of underworld and Heavenly secrets.

Nope, Azagoth didn't give a shit about any of that. What he cared about was getting his emotions under control and his life in order. He didn't know how to deal with his rogue emotions, but he did have an idea about the rest.

Unfortunately, that meant dealing with the Memitim Council, and for some reason, the only people ever appointed to the Council hated him.

For thousands of years he'd kept out of their business, letting them govern the Memitim in whatever shortsighted, dumbass manner they saw fit.

But those days were over. Azagoth had been absent as a parent, very hands-off, and as a result, his children had suffered.

There was a tap at the door, and his assistant, Zhubaal, entered. "My lord, Mariella is here."

"It's about fucking time," he snarled. "Send her in."

The tall, elegant brunette swept into his office, her purple velvet robes swishing around her high-heeled, jewel-encrusted shoes, her cinnamon wings extended and puffed up, as if she expected a fight.

It wasn't as if a fight would be completely unprecedented.

Azagoth despised angels. Most of them, anyway. But the worst of the very worst were those who looked down their heavenly noses at him. Oh, they respected his power and his position, but on a personal level, they thought he was scum.

Mariella, in particular, thought he was a supreme lowlife, and she had for the entire three centuries in which she'd been his primary Heavenly liaison.

He *hated* her.

He glared as she launched into a tirade, lecturing him about his duties that related to Memitim. Thing was, she'd never been Memitim, wasn't on the Council, and she didn't even work in the embassy. She should be lecturing him about anything *but* Memitim.

"In summary," she said, "you are out of luck."

For the millionth time he thought about tossing her into the tunnel behind the wall panel and sending her to play with millions of demon souls. Just five minutes in the Inner Sanctum would wipe that smug look off her face. But it wouldn't get him what he wanted.

Be civil. "I'm not asking for the Memitim program to end," he gritted out. "I'm asking for some changes."

"No."

"Dammit, let me speak to someone on the fucking council."

"Azagoth, you agreed to this thousands of years ago. You signed a contract in blood. And now, with fewer Memitim than ever, it's even more crucial that the rules be strictly followed."

"Oh, fuck off," he snapped. "There's no shortage of Memitim."

"You have stopped fathering them, have you not?"

Stupid question, because she knew the damned answer. "You know I did, a couple of years ago when I took Lilliana as my mate. But that's hardly enough time for Memitim numbers to suffer."

She shook her head. "Production started going down centuries ago," she said, making it sound like Azagoth had been putting his children together on an assembly line. "We used to get seventy-two Memitim from you per year. But even as the human population exploded and increased the need for guardians, you slowed down. Started refusing the females sent to you. You used to be so...prolific."

That was because he used to believe in the cause. And he'd been young, dumb, and horny. Oh, and evil. Very evil. Then, sometime around the Industrial Revolution, he'd begun to grow bitter and angry. Rebellious. And it had been extremely satisfying to refuse the angels sent to his bed.

Still, he'd always left Memitim business to the Memitim Council. Until recently. Recently...he'd mated Lilliana. He'd filled his realm with his offspring and had gotten to know them. He'd also lost some who had died in battle protecting their Primori. And just this year, three others, mere children, had lost their lives growing up in horrible human conditions.

Oh, yeah, it was time for some shit to change, and he was done being civil.

"Listen to me," he snarled as he backed her against the door he was going to toss her out of. "On some items there is room for negotiation. Then there are the things I *demand*. No negotiating on those."

"Like plucking your juvenile offspring out of the human world and bringing them to you? Or taking your daughter Suzanne out of the Memitim program?"

"Yes, and yes. My children should grow up here, and Suzanne, despite being assigned a Primori, isn't suited for this life."

"That's for the Memitim Council to decide. Not you."

Murderous desire made his fangs throb for a taste of angel blood. "She's my daughter!"

"She's an instrument of Heaven, created by you for that purpose." Mariella's mouth twisted in distaste, as if she was picturing lying with him in bed. "You waived all rights to fatherhood the moment you spilled your seed inside her mother. You're lucky we allowed you to open Sheoul-gra to your adult offspring. There's no way you're taking control of the juveniles."

Cold, seething anger congealed in his veins. He did *not* like to be told no.

"Send me a Council member," he growled. "I'm done with you."

Her chin tilted up in defiance, but her lower lip trembled. Good. More of her was going to be trembling if he didn't get his way.

"Council members aren't authorized to negotiate with you."

"Send one!" he roared, his patience shredded. "Send one *today*."

"I'll see what I can do."

Satisfied—for now—he released the angel.

But if he didn't see a Memitim Council member soon, Heaven was going to get a taste of his brand of hell.

* * * *

Lilliana drained her wine glass as if an instruction manual that would explain her mate was at the bottom.

One wasn't.

"Was that weird?" Idess asked as she refilled her own glass. "Because I feel like that was weird."

Lilliana sighed. "It was weird. I'm sorry, Idess. He's been moody lately."

"Is something going on?"

"I don't know." Lilliana smiled at Mace as he chased a butterfly. "He won't talk to me about it."

She'd tried on several occasions to get him to discuss whatever was making him grumpy, but he'd always either changed the subject or distracted her...usually with sex.

"Is there anything I can do to help?" Idess asked. "I'm not that close to him, but I could try talking to him."

"I think you're closer to him than any of his children," Lilliana said. "But you know, I think that might be part of the issue. He's been spending more time with all of his sons and daughters. I've even heard him asking them about their pasts. Maybe he's been trying to get closer to them."

Idess smiled. "He's opened up so much since you came into his life."

"Lately it doesn't feel that way." No, it felt like he was pulling away from her. "And I don't understand. Things are going so well here. I thought he was happy."

"I'm sure he is." Idess covered Lilliana's hand with hers. "Whatever is going on with him isn't about you."

"I hope you're right." But secretly, Lilliana wasn't so sure. She *was* certain he'd been avoiding her, but why? A group of Memitim walked by, arms loaded with party supplies. The two males and one of the females gave her an awkward wave or a smile, but the other two, a male and female, ignored her while waving to Idess. Lilliana got along with most of Azagoth's offspring, but a handful despised her, or Azagoth, or both of them, and nothing she ever did made a difference. "Are you planning to stay for the festivities?"

Idess frowned. "Festivities?"

"It's The Celebration of Angels Day."

"Ah, yes." Idess rolled her eyes. "The day angels everywhere get to congratulate themselves on being awesome and powerful and better than all other living things."

"Precisely."

Lilliana grinned at the other female. She adored Idess and wished they could spend more time together. Unfortunately, Idess was busy with her family and her work at Underworld General, where she escorted human souls into the Heavenly light, and Lilliana was, with few, specific exceptions, restricted to Sheoul-gra.

"I wish I could, but I need to be at a baby shower in an hour. Thanatos's mate, Regan, is pregnant with their second child."

Thanatos, one of the legendary Four Horsemen of the Apocalypse, had come to Azagoth once for a favor, but that was before Lilliana's time, and she'd never met the guy or his ex-demon slayer mate.

"Send them my best," Lilliana said, struggling to conceal the wistfulness in her voice.

She'd never expected anything even close to a traditional life with Azagoth, but sometimes hearing how normal things could be, even for biblical legends, made her a little envious.

Would anyone hold a baby shower for her baby when the time came? Would Azagoth even be excited, given that their child would be only one of thousands?

"Hey," Idess said softly. "Are you okay?"

"I'm fine," Lilliana said, and she was.

Really. She was a little tired, maybe, and if she was honest with herself, she'd say she was a bit lonely. Whatever was going on with Azagoth had taken him away from her, not just emotionally, but physically, too.

Well, except when it came to sex. Which, she just realized, might be the key to getting him to talk. She just had to go about it in a different way.

With a shaking hand, she poured another glass of liquid resolve.

Azagoth was about to get a lesson in abstinence, and he was very much not fond of being told no.

Chapter Seven

Sheoul-gra, and all its ancient Greek glory, was teeming with activity when Hawkyn arrived. It took a minute to figure out why colorful paper lights had been strung up between trees and buildings, food and drink had been set out on dozens of long trestle tables, and music was being streamed via magical conduits that dispersed sound evenly throughout the entire realm.

It was The Celebration of Angels Day, a holiday he figured had been invented to let typically uptight angels release a little pressure. Rumor had it that angels could do whatever they wanted on this day and there would be no repercussions.

Hawkyn wasn't going to take that chance.

"Hey, man." Cipher, his long blond hair tied back with a strip of leather, clapped him on the shoulder and drained a cup of mead. The Unfallen angel loved his nasty ancient beverages. "Where've you been?"

Journey flanked his other side. "Dude, you were gone for days."

"Days, dude," Maddox agreed as he stumbled alongside Journey. Hawk had known Maddox for over a hundred years, and although his brother was older by twenty years, he still acted like a delinquent teen human.

"What, you guys are my babysitters now?"

Cipher snagged another cup of mead off a nearby table. "You missed game night."

"And movie night," Journey chimed in. "We watched John Wick."

"The second one," Mad added. "It was awesome. If that character was real, he'd totally be Primori."

"I'll bet Keanu Reeves is," Cipher said. "He's had a big impact on society."

"I heard he's a vampire. Or a demon." Maddox gestured at the nearby gazebo. "And speaking of demons, you just missed Idess. Well, you missed her by a couple of hours, I guess."

Cipher braced his shoulder against a marble column, propping the heel of his boot on the snout of a demon carved into the base. "Who's Idess?"

"Of all my father's children," Hawkyn said, "she's his favorite." He waved to his half-brother Emerico, who headed their way.

Journey snorted. "You could have fooled me."

"What do you mean?"

"She came to see him with her demon kid, but he barely spoke to her. Totally ignored her demonlet, and then he took off. Left Idess with Lilliana. Our father can be a dick sometimes."

"Sometimes?" Emerico joined them, his spiky black hair looking like something out of a cartoon. "He's a fucking career dick. I asked him why we can't enter the Inner Sanctum and he said he doesn't trust us. Like we're children. Bastard."

"Shh." Mad looked around wildly and lowered his voice. "He'll hear you."

"I don't give a shit," Journey said, all puffed up like a rooster. "I've told him the same thing to his face."

"To his face?" Hawkyn was more than a little skeptical.

"Well, I've said it on the Memitim message boards," Journey muttered, and yeah, that was more like it.

Maddox hiccupped. "You're a bully."

Cipher shook his head. "Bullying requires a power imbalance, real or perceived, in favor of the bully. Azagoth has all the power. Journey has none. Plus, Azagoth doesn't know what Journey says on the boards. Hence, no bullying." He punched Journey in the arm. "I think you mean he's a troll. An idiot troll, but not a bully."

"Okay, guys, can we get serious for a second?"

Abruptly, Journey lost the swagger and cocky grin. The guy could switch into duty mode faster than anyone Hawkyn had met. "What's up?"

"You watched over two serial killers in your life—"

"Three." Journey ticked off his fingers as he spoke. "Plus an assortment of rapists, sadists, mass murderers, and even an emperor who regularly ordered the executions of entire villages of people."

Yeah, Hawkyn had been assigned a variety of monsters too, but for some reason, serial killers like Drayger seemed extra monstrous. The time they took to plan and execute their evil put them ahead of the rest, in his opinion.

"How do you deal with it?" Cipher asked. "I know you're not allowed to interfere in your Primoris' lives, but fuck that, man. How can you just let someone be tortured to death by one of your Primori?"

"Those people are dying for the greater good," Journey said, reciting the official company line like a good little soldier. "It's why they were born. They have a purpose to serve. And it helps to realize that their suffering is temporary. A drop in the bucket of time. They go to a better place."

Maddox jammed his hands into his jeans' pockets. "It also helps to avoid your scumbag Primori. Don't even check on them unless their *heraldis* activate." He shrugged. "Ignorance is bliss, you know."

"Preach it, brother." Emerico bumped fists with Maddox.

It was way too late to be ignorant about Drayger. Besides, Hawkyn *wanted* to learn about his charges. The more he knew about their lives and their personalities, the easier it was to understand why they required angelic protection and from where any danger might come. Hawk had never understood why people like Maddox and Rico treated their jobs so casually. Hawkyn had always been dedicated to a fault, an all-in kind of Memitim.

"I can't do that," he said. "Especially now. I kind of fucked up."

Cipher shoved away from the column, his interest fully engaged. "Ooh, do tell. It's always good to have dirt on you."

Cipher hadn't changed a bit since the day, almost two years ago, when Hawkyn had dragged the guy here against his will for fucking with another of Hawkyn's Primoris. Ciph was still a bit of a scammer. But he did have a moral compass, and despite their rocky start, they'd become good friends, and Hawkyn trusted him with his secrets.

Journey and Maddox were a little more iffy, but they were his favorite brothers and he didn't think they'd betray him.

Probably.

Emerico? He'd been raised by professional con artists, and while he was generally reliable, he tended to look for all the angles in any situation that would benefit him.

Ah, what the hell. Hawkyn needed advice, and these four idiots were the best source of it he had. "I interfered with my Primori's abduction of a victim," he blurted.

Journey let out a drawn out *oh shit* whistle. "Dude."

Maddox concurred. "Dude."

Rico did a face palm.

"I know I'm not up on all your crazy Primori rules," Cipher began, "but even I know that interference in Primori actions is crazy bad. Like, the most forbidden of the forbidden."

"There's worse," Hawkyn said, "but not much."

"So what happened?" Journey asked, his dark eyes wide with morbid curiosity. Because who didn't love a good train wreck?

"I'm fucked, that's what happened." Hawk swiped a cup of wine from the table and drained half of it. He wasn't much of a drinker, but he could use some alcohol right now. Good thing wine was approved by the Memitim Council, because he was tempted to drink it by the barrel. "I caught him trying to grab a woman. She mistook me for his partner, and she blasted the fuck out of me with a photon torpedo or some crap before he managed to subdue her."

"Ah, shit," Maddox said. "So did you take damage meant for him?"

"I don't know. That's what I'm worried about." Hawkyn looked at each of his buddies and wondered who was going to freak the most when he said, "So I rescued her."

"Holy shit," Maddox blurted, spewing wine all over Hawk's boots.

Groaning, Journey scrubbed his hand over his face. "You dipshit. You fucking dipshit."

Rico gaped. His eyes were going to dry out if he didn't blink.

Cipher stood silently, his gaze analyzing Hawkyn's words, expression, posture... The guy was a master at reading people. No doubt he knew exactly how much shit Hawkyn was in. "What are you going to do?"

"I don't know."

"Take her back," Rico suggested, as if Drayger's House of Horrors had a return policy.

"You're an idiot," Cipher said. "Even if Hawk did that, there's no guarantee that it'll repair the fated timeline. Like Maddox said, what if she was supposed to have killed the Primori? She never would have been taken. He could be returning her to a killer for no reason." He looked at Hawkyn. "Man, you're fucked."

"Thank you," Hawkyn muttered. "That was helpful."

"You said it first." Cipher shrugged. "So what is your plan?"

"I don't have one. Which is why I'm talking to you guys. But, as it turns out, you're idiots."

"Well," Journey began, "can you contact the Memitim Council and see what they know about your Primori's fate?"

"I tried. Talked to someone from the embassy. Got nowhere."

"Is your Primori human?" Rico asked.

That was the question of the day. "I'm not sure. The files and diary Atticus kept on him before he Ascended indicates that Drayger's human, but he can somehow track his victims once he sheds their blood. Atticus wrote that a victim escaped, but she didn't go to the police because she was a werewolf and she feared being caught." A lot of cops were secret Aegis members, so the victim's paranoia was justified. "Instead, she used a Harrowgate to go from Portland to Sydney, and the bastard caught up to her within days."

Atticus had spent every available minute watching Drayger, documenting his every move. For some reason Atticus had been obsessed with the bastard. He might have even admired him. The diary he'd kept had been detailed and often complimentary.

He has a single-minded focus. He can't sleep or eat. His only desire is to find Lexi. He took leave from work. Spends his time hunched over his computer and a giant map of the world. He's looking for her.

Next entry: *Jason Drayger is fascinating. Everything I've learned about the man leads me to believe he's human, and yet he can sense supernatural abilities in females. (But not males.) And as far as I can tell, he can track anything once he tastes their blood. I'm certain that he practiced many times before Lexi escaped and forced him to hunt her. I think he'll find her.*

Several entries and two days later later: *He found her.*

Lexi's death photos now took up five pages in Drayger's serial killer album.

"So you're left with a choice," Cipher mused. "Leave her be and see if he catches her and the fated timeline fixes itself, or protect her to keep her out of his hands in case she wasn't meant to be a victim."

"Exactly. And if he can track her, I'll have to make sure I keep her someplace where he can't sense her or where he can't access her even if he does find her." He could bring her here, he supposed, just until he could figure out what to do next.

He'd just have to be sneaky about it, because no one besides these four morons could know what was up. Not even Suzanne could know. He trusted her, but he was her mentor, and he couldn't hold the moral high ground if she knew he'd buried himself six feet deep. He was in a definite *do as I say, not as I do* moment.

He was so fucked.

"Sucks to be you," Cipher said, his nose in the air as he sniffed out the charcoal aroma of something being grilled nearby.

"Says the guy who got his wings cut off and his ass booted out of Heaven." Maddox dug a Sheoulin coin out of his pocket and flipped it into the nearby fountain that had run with blood for thousands of years before Lilliana tamed Azagoth's inner demon. Two seconds later, the fangfish that lived in the fountain spit the coin out.

"My punishment was totally unfair," Cipher muttered as he snatched the coin out of the air.

Hawkyn stared at his friend in disbelief. "You seduced my Primori, which affected her status and left a big black mark on my record."

"I didn't know she was a Primori when I seduced her."

"Bullshit. I told you."

"Sure you did." Cipher's gaze locked on a female Unfallen standing near the newly constructed stage that would soon be the battle ground for a band competition, and later, for wrestling matches—except these matches were fought with the mind. "*After* I decided I wanted her."

"It didn't matter, you jackass. She was human. Angels are forbidden from sleeping with humans."

"Wrong. She was part angel." If the heat in his gaze was any indication, Cipher probably had that Unfallen across the way half undressed in his head by now.

"Yeah, like from ten generations ago."

"See? Part angel."

"And did that argument work during your sentencing?"

"No," he conceded, finally turning back to Hawk. "But archangels are assholes."

Hawkyn wasn't going to argue with that assessment. "Look, I need help. I'm open to suggestions."

"Bring her here for now. She'll be safe. Then we can look at ways to get you out of this mess." Cipher could be an immature whack job at times, but when shit hit the fan, he could always be counted on to help clean it up.

"Okay—" He broke off as the ground beneath them rumbled, and a charge in the air made Hawkyn's hair stand up. "Uh-oh."

"What is it?" Cipher asked.

"Azagoth." Everyone had stopped what they were doing as a blast of fury blew like a shockwave across the land. Glass shattered and pillars tipped over, and oh, shit, this could be bad.

As a group, Hawkyn, Cipher, Journey, and Maddox ran toward the epicenter of the rumbling—the portal to and from Sheoul-gra.

Hawkyn looked back over his shoulder at Rico, who was staring down at the *heraldis* on his arm. He flashed out, most likely to defend a Primori. Hawkyn sped up, beating the group before skidding to a halt at the sight of Azagoth, his eyes glowing like hot lava and his skin threaded with black, pulsing veins. In his clawed hand, he held a ruby-winged angel by her throat.

"Don't fuck with me, Ulnara," he snarled. "I. Want. My. Children!"

Ulnara? Hawkyn sucked in a harsh breath. Ulnara was his mother's name. The female struggling to escape Azagoth's grip, the female with Suzanne's brown hair and eyes and Hawkyn's nose *was his mother.*

She laughed, a raspy, choking sound that was no surprise given that Azagoth had a death grip on her neck.

"As if you care about your children. This?" She waved her arm in an encompassing gesture. "All of this is either a show or a means to an end that will benefit only you. Do any of them actually believe you love them? Are you even capable of love, you evil maggot?"

"I'm far more capable of it than you are," he yelled, slamming her against a nearby pillar. Feathers floated in the air around them as her wings, pinned between the stone column and her body, flapped uselessly. "You will convince the Council to give me what I want, and you'll do it now."

"Or what?"

Azagoth let out a roar of fury. Wet, ripping noises rent the air as his body morphed into something bigger, with horns and scales and black, leathery wings tipped with serrated bone hooks. He flung the angel away from the pillar and snapped his massive jaws mere millimeters from her face.

"Father, no!" Hawkyn had never met his mother, hadn't thought he ever would. But that was her. He was sure of it. And he had to stop Azagoth from killing her.

He charged, slamming full force into the Azagoth-demon and knocking him sideways. Azagoth released Ulnara, and in a motion so seamless and instantaneous that Hawkyn didn't have a chance to avoid it, he popped Hawk in the throat and power-slammed him into the ground.

The air whooshed from his lungs from both the impact and the giant, clawed foot on his chest. Azagoth looked down at him, drool dripping from a mouthful of teeth a dragon would envy, and snarled.

"Today is not the day to piss me off." He spun around and jabbed one long finger at Ulnara. "You can thank our son for saving you from all the screaming you were about to do." He flapped his wings and launched into the air, where he hovered about thirty feet up. "Ulnara, you have one week."

She scrambled onto the portal pad, her hand poised over the hilt of the sword at her hip. An instinct and nothing more, because she had to realize that no blade could so much as scratch Azagoth. Not in his own realm, and certainly not while he was wearing his demon suit.

"Not this time, Azagoth," she said, her voice powerful and confident, but she never took her nervous gaze off the demon in the air. "We're done appeasing you."

"Don't test my will, angel," he warned, his voice dredging the very pits of hell. "On this matter I will go to war."

War? What the hell was going on?

Azagoth flicked his wrist, done with her. Literally. She disappeared without ever activating the portal, returned either to Heaven, or dumped somewhere that amused Azagoth. Like inside a sewer treatment holding tank. Or a hot dog factory.

Without bothering to even glance at Hawkyn, Azagoth flapped his great wings and shot skyward, vanishing into roiling clouds that hadn't been there a moment ago.

"Well," Cipher drawled as he offered Hawkyn a hand, "at least you're consistent, always rescuing females from crazy males."

"No matter how stupid it is," Maddox said.

Journey shook his head. "I can't believe you fucking did that."

Hawk couldn't either. "The angel was my mother."

Cipher cocked a blond eyebrow, and both Journey and Maddox gasped out loud.

"Damn," Journey said. "I've never met any Memitim dam, let alone mine."

"No one has," Maddox said.

"Would you want to?" Cipher asked, and both Journey and Maddox shook their heads.

After all, what did one say to the female who gave you up, not for your own good, but because you were a means to an end, a pawn in a game you were bred to play whether you wanted to or not?

"Hawkyn!" Lilliana jogged over, fingers playing with the ends of the long blond braid draped over her shoulder. "I saw what happened. Are you okay?" At his nod, she smiled and dropped her hands to her sides. "Good. Next question. Are you completely stupid?"

He glanced at his friends, who were nodding vehemently. "The consensus seems to be yes." He glared at all the onlookers, shaming them into heading back to whatever they'd been doing before he tackled his father. "What did Azagoth mean by going to war?" he asked Lilliana. "Over what? The children he was talking about?" And what children?

"I don't know." She crossed her arms over her chest, ruffling her silky blue blouse. "I have no idea what's going on with Azagoth, but you all need to tread softly around him for a while. I haven't seen him this volatile since I first arrived in Sheoul-gra. He loves you—all of you—but I think he might have loved some of the people he turned into living statues, too."

"Does he?" Journey asked quietly. "Does he really?"

Lilliana frowned. "Does he what? Love some of the statues?"

"No. Love us."

"Of course he does," she said, but Hawkyn swore he heard a note of doubt in her voice.

Maddox snorted. "He's an angel wrapped in a demon wrapped in an asshole. He doesn't give a shit about anything but himself."

In an instant Lilliana was in Maddox's face, her eyes glowing with anger, her wings, which Hawkyn had never seen, held high, engulfing his brother in shadow. She was shorter than Maddox by at least six inches, but somehow she seemed to tower over him.

"How dare you, you ungrateful wretch," she snapped, compelling Mad backward with the force of her anger. Anger Hawk hadn't known she was capable of. Lilliana had always been so calm and sweet. "Do you not see what he's done for you? For all of you? Are you completely blind to what he's built here for you? He didn't do it for show or personal or political gain, no matter what Ulnara said. I saw his misery and felt his pain when your brother Methicore managed to shut down Sheoul-gra to Memitim access a while back. But your father called in about a million favors to have the decision reversed—favors that cost him dearly." She jammed her finger into Maddox's chest. "So if you can't show him a little respect, I will personally show you the door."

Maddox held up his hands in surrender, but he was careful not to spill the wine in one hand.

"Yes, ma'am," he said meekly. "I apologize."

For a long moment, Hawkyn wasn't sure she was going to accept his apology, but just as he was weighing ways to de-escalate the situation, she stepped back with an irritated flap of wings.

"Good," she said crisply. "Now, I'm going to go check on him. You boys enjoy the party."

Hawkyn assured her he would, but he didn't plan to stay. He needed to go over the notes he had about Drayger's past, and then he had to figure out what to do with Aurora.

He was about to wave off his buddies when his arm seized up and pain shot from his wrist to his shoulder. Hissing, he looked down at the row of seven *heraldis* that extended from the heel of his hand to the crook of his elbow. The one in the middle was pulsing, red, angry.

One of his Primoris was in trouble.

"I got your back," Journey said. "Let's go."

"I'm in," Cipher said. "Let's kick ass."

Maddox downed his wine and threw the cup down on the ground

like a victory spike. "Kick ass!"

Hawkyn would sideline Maddox's drunk butt if he needed to, but for now he was just happy to have friends and family at his back.

On this matter, I will go to war.

Especially now.

Chapter Eight

Reaching for the door handle to Azagoth's office, Lilliana took a deep, bracing breath. But as her hand closed on the cold metal, she hesitated. She'd seen her mate in rages before, and she knew to give him space. Lots of space. Especially after he lost control of his inner demon and let it loose to play.

She glanced at her watch. It had been an hour since he'd flown away in a huff. She'd never even seen him fly before. What did it mean? What was going on with him?

Her gut churned as she steadied herself with one final mental pep talk and opened the door.

He'd returned to his usual handsome form, standing so close to the fireplace that flames licked at the hem of the black robe he must have thrown on after shifting out of his beast form, which generally destroyed his clothing.

"Hey," she said softly.

His big body shuddered, but he didn't turn around. "My love."

Every time he called her that, she melted a little inside. She'd originally come to Sheoul-gra to steal something from him, and he liked to claim that what she stole was his heart. He'd stolen hers, too, and even when things were rough, she still felt like the luckiest angel ever.

The door closed behind her with a muffled thud. "Are you okay?"

"Yes."

Ignoring what was obviously a lie, she moved closer. "I'm worried about you. You've been so cranky and distant."

"It's nothing." He turned to her, affecting a smile that was clearly meant to placate her. "Just work stuff."

"I think it's more than that." She rested her hand on his arm. "Please, darling. Let me in."

He let out a low, seductive growl and tugged her to him. "How about you let *me* in..."

Always before when he touched her like this she'd given in. But not this time.

"No." Gently, she shoved him away. "You aren't going to distract me again. I want to know what set you off today. I also want to know more about the angel you were fighting with."

Lilliana had never been jealous of his past lovers, mainly because she knew that most of them had viewed him only as a means to reproduce, a duty and a sacrifice. But she'd also never expected any of them to come to Sheoul-gra now that he was mated. Clearly Ulnara hated him, and he didn't appear to be overly fond of her, either, but hearing him say that she could thank *their* son for saving her had been like a punch to the stomach.

"What set me off," he growled, "is that the Memitim Council is refusing to reveal the locations of any of my young children who are still living among the humans."

She blinked in confusion. "Why do you want to know where they are? You've never known, have you?"

"No, I haven't. But I want to know now." His smoky emerald gaze locked with hers. "And I want them brought here."

Whoa. She sucked in a startled breath. This was...unexpected. Long overdue, perhaps, but unexpected nevertheless. Especially given the fact that he'd said he wasn't ready for he and Lilliana to have children. Yet now he wanted scores of them, the ones he'd made with other females, to fill his realm?

"How long have you been wanting this to happen? And why didn't you tell me?" She tried not to be upset by the fact that he hadn't discussed this with her, but it was impossible to keep the thread of hurt out of her voice.

"A while," he said, and if he was aware on any level that she felt bruised by his lack of disclosure, it didn't show. "I didn't tell you because I didn't want to say anything until I knew it was even a possibility. Which it doesn't appear to be."

"Why would they refuse you? Especially since our mating changed how Memitim are created, right?"

"Precisely," he growled. "It's bullshit. New Memitim class angels can now be born to any Heavenly angel. And unlike my offspring, they won't be abandoned for humans to raise. They'll be raised and trained in Heaven like normal angels of all classes and Orders."

"So why was Ulnara here?"

"Because she's on the Council now."

She frowned. "Shouldn't members of the Memitim Council be Memitim?"

"You'd think. But that rule has been changed, because apparently now that Memitim can be born to Heavenly angels, Heavenly angels get to rule."

Lilliana didn't like that one bit. "So that means you'll be seeing more of your ex-lovers?"

"I hope not."

Right there with ya.

Frustrated but not wanting to dwell on Azagoth's ex-lovers, she changed the subject. "Look, why don't we forget about all of this for a while? We haven't used the *chronoglass* to go anywhere in weeks. Let's visit a tropical beach or a mountain meadow. We can have a picnic, some wine...and we can talk."

Her ability to time travel and take him anywhere in the world for one hour every twenty-four was a gift they'd used almost daily for their entire relationship...until a few weeks ago when he'd suddenly become "too busy."

He waggled his brows playfully. "You know if we go someplace romantic like that, we won't be *talking*."

"Yes, we will," she said firmly. "I'm not falling for your erotic tricks, Azagoth. Not until you tell me what's up with you." She held up a finger to cut him off before he said what she knew he was going to say. "And don't tell me it's nothing. I know that's not the truth."

The temperature in the room plummeted so low she could see her breath. But not her husband's. No, he'd gone so cold his breath wouldn't be visible even in Antarctica.

"Are you calling me a liar?"

Annoyed by his sudden mood swing and tired of trying to get him to talk, she let out a bitter laugh.

"Seriously? You cause pain and suffering every day. You scheme with evil demons and plot with angels. And you're going to feign outrage at being called a liar? Especially when it's the truth? You're angry that I'm not dumb enough to believe your denials, is that it? Or are you mad at yourself for not being a better liar? Either way, knock it off. You're a bazillion years old. Act like it. Man up."

She knew the moment she stopped talking that she'd gone too far. Azagoth's eyes went glacial for a split-second before they flared hot, orange flames lapping at his irises.

"I love you," he said in a deep, tortured voice. "So you should go."

As angry as she was, as sure as she was that she was the one who was in the right, she also knew that if she wanted to win the war, she had to strategically retreat from certain battles. Azagoth wouldn't hurt her physically, she knew that without a doubt, but he was more demon than angel, and when the angel inside him fled, the demon that remained could flay her alive with his words. Staying here would only lead to pain for them both and no one would win.

She glanced at her watch. "I have things to do. But Azagoth, we aren't done with this conversation."

She slammed out of his office, and as she walked down the endless hallway, his roar of anger echoed off the walls, jiggling the chandeliers and rattling the artwork.

But nothing was more rattled than her nerves.

Chapter Nine

It took longer than Hawk wanted to put down the threat to his endangered Primori, a member of the Demonic Activity Response Team, whom he'd been guarding since he was born. Jake Biemer had originally joined The Aegis, a demon-slaying organization, following a stint in the navy. But a few years ago, when The Aegis took a new, radical stance he didn't like, he'd joined the other Aegis defectors to start DART. Now the guy spent his time investigating demonic activity that put him in danger all the time. Fortunately, Hawk only had to respond to dangers that were somehow not fated to happen.

Seemed like ever since the near-apocalypse several years ago, non-fated danger happened far more than it ever had.

And Hawk wasn't the only one who noticed. Most of his Memitim brethren had complained of the same thing. It was as if the glue that held all the laws of nature together had started to dissolve, leaving weak spots everywhere. Even Sheoul-gra's Inner Sanctum where the souls were kept wasn't immune. Azagoth and Hades had been dealing with cracks in the containment walls that hadn't been there before.

And naturally, no one in Heaven would offer any explanations.

It was one of the reasons Hawk couldn't wait to Ascend. He wanted to get answers and then he wanted to share those answers with his brothers and sisters. He wanted to make life better for Memitim, and better for the decent people they protected. To be included on the Memitim Council was his goal, and dammit, he would reach it.

But that wasn't going to happen if he failed to keep a Primori safe. Even the pieces of shit like Drayger.

Crisis averted, Hawk said goodbye to Cipher and his brothers and headed back to Underworld General. He didn't have a plan for Aurora yet—he only knew he had to convince her not to go to the police.

"Hey, I know the guy tortured you and was planning to kill you slowly, but really, is forgiving and forgetting too much to ask?"

Yeah, that was going to go over real well.

In what was becoming a routine, he flashed himself to the hospital, entered through the ER doors from the parking lot, and approached the reception desk.

"Can I help you?" The chick at the reception desk looked at him with beady, unblinking eyes.

"I'm here to see Aurora Mercer. She was admitted yesterday."

The demon tapped a few keys on her computer keyboard. "I'm sorry, but she's been released."

"What? When?"

"Three hours ago."

"Three hours?" Drayger could have her again by now. "What the hell? Why didn't anyone notify me?"

She scowled at the screen. "Did you leave contact information?"

"Yes."

"Did you leave instructions to be notified of any change in her status?"

Shit. He'd taken off too quickly to even think about that. "Ah, no."

She smiled sweetly. "Then apologize for yelling at me or kindly fuck off."

"You know, your staff's reputation for rudeness is legendary, but that was almost pleasant."

"Doctor Eidolon asked us to be nicer."

Hawkyn doubted that "be nicer" meant that the staff was supposed to smile while telling people to fuck off, but whatever.

"Oh, well, then I apologize, and I'll be sure to tell Eidolon that you're making a great effort."

Ignoring her legitimately dubious snort, he went out to the parking lot and flashed himself to Aurora's house, thankful he'd scoped it out earlier, or he'd have had to waste valuable time finding it.

He materialized in front of the house, his shadow wings deployed and keeping him invisible to all but other Memitim.

It was late afternoon in Portland, the sun hidden behind a thick layer of low clouds. The damp ground smelled like dirt and moss, but he also caught a whiff of something sweet from the bakery down the block. Aurora lived in a nice neighborhood, one that was probably considered safe.

He moved down her narrow walkway toward the front steps and her tiny brick-colored porch, which was barely large enough for the two small chairs and folding table she'd put there. He could have materialized inside her house, but that would be rude. And stalker-y. Plus, given the trauma she'd already endured, it would be a serious asshole move that would probably terrify her.

He'd just ring the doorbell.

How quaint.

* * * *

Aurora knew she shouldn't be at her house, given that a serial killer had her address and would almost certainly try to silence her. But she didn't have anyplace else to go where she wouldn't put friends and family in danger. What she did have was an arsenal of mystical weapons and deterrents, and she'd gathered just enough energy from the hospital staff to deploy them.

The nice werewolf lady named Runa who had escorted her home had unintentionally provided a strong surge of power when she'd given her a hug, allowing Aurora's palm to linger on her back. Runa wouldn't miss the stolen energy, but it had gone a long way toward filling Aurora's empty well.

In any case, she didn't plan to be in danger for long. She was going to the police as soon as she could come up with a plausible story for her escape and lack of injuries. After all, Underworld General's medical staff had done an amazing job of healing her. During the long, hot shower she'd taken within seconds of getting home, she'd noticed that the scar on her thigh was barely noticeable, and all the other bruises, cuts, and abrasions were gone entirely. A demon dentist had even fixed the tooth the bastard had nearly knocked out.

The microwave dinged, announcing that her mac and cheese was ready. What she wouldn't give for a good plate of homemade pasta—not that she could cook worth a damn—but she was exhausted and would just have to settle for frozen stuff from a box. At least it was organic.

Inhaling the mouthwatering aroma of cheesy goodness, she headed toward the kitchen but without warning, the hair on the back of her neck stood up. Her protective ward had triggered.

A split second later, she heard the deep voice that had filled her ears during her dreams.

"*What the fuck?*"

Oh, shit. She ran to the window and pulled back the cheery yellow curtains that perfectly matched the floral pattern on her steel blue sofa. And there, standing motionless, arms pinned to his side on her doorstep, was the man—no, the *angel*—who had saved her life.

She didn't bother to slip on shoes. She scrambled to open the door and nearly tripped over her own bare feet in her haste to get outside.

"Hey," Hawkyn said through clenched teeth. "Nice security system you've got here. Could do without the electrical current frying my insides, though."

"Yeah, well, it wasn't meant for you." She closed her eyes and concentrated on the low-level vibration emanating from the trap she'd set. An invisible thread of energy, much like a power cord, stretched from her to the protective bubble around the house, and with a whispered command, "Rojalis," it snapped.

Instantly, Hawkyn relaxed, taking in gulps of air, his broad chest heaving under his black turtleneck and leather jacket. Damn, he was magnificent, his long, lean thighs encased in dark jeans that bunched around well-used combat boots. She never would have guessed he was an angel, but damn, it was a good look, and despite the horror of the past days, her body grew uncomfortably warm.

Damn her succubus genes.

"That was unpleasant," he said in a deep, husky voice that turned up the temperature even more, "and I'm an *angel*. What the hell would happen to a human who got caught in your trap?"

"A good human?" She shrugged. "Nothing. The trap was calibrated for evil." She paused, an icy finger of fear poking her in the libido, and she took a casual step back in case she needed to slam the door in his face. "Um, if you're an angel, why would it snare you?"

"Long sto—"

"Don't," she broke in with a wag of her finger. "Don't even go there."

One blond eyebrow arched high, and she suspected he wasn't used to being cut off.

"Okay, short story it is." He jammed his hands in his jacket pockets. "My dad is evil. Sort of."

Well, that wasn't expected. "Isn't your dad, uh, God?"

"No."

"All right, then. I have a lot to learn." She gestured in invitation. "Want to come in? Do you need permission?"

One corner of his mouth tipped up in amusement. "I'm an angel, not a vampire from some campy movie." His voice, just like at the hospital, was so whiskey smooth she thought she could get drunk from merely listening to him.

"Well, you *do* have fangs," she pointed out, feeling a little foolish.

He chuckled, but his boots didn't make a sound on her hardwood floors as he walked inside, surprising from such a large male. She closed the door behind him and reached deep for her power, but now that the trap had been triggered and shut down, she didn't have enough left to set it again. Well, she supposed that if worst came to worst, the angel standing in her living room would be adequate protection from the psychopath who'd tried to kill her.

"I'm sorry I wasn't there when you were released from the hospital." He swung around to her, more muscle and hotness than had ever been in her home. "I assume you took a Harrowgate home?"

"Yes," she said, without elaborating. He didn't need to know that her people couldn't see, and therefore use, Harrowgates like normal underworlders could. That little tidbit of info could stay between her and Runa, who *had* been able to use the Harrowgate to get Aurora from New York to Portland in a matter of seconds. "And it's perfectly fine that you weren't there. You aren't my caretaker." She maneuvered around him to get to the kitchen. "Can I offer you a drink or anything?"

"No, thank you." He followed her, his presence making her six hundred square foot home feel even more like a shoebox than it already did. "How are you doing?"

As long as she didn't think about what had happened to her, she was A-okay. "I'll be better once I go to the police."

"Ah, yeah." He raked his fingers through his hair and looked at everything but her. "That's the thing. You can't go to them."

She pulled her macaroni and cheese from the microwave. "Excuse me? Why not?" When he didn't answer, she slammed the microwave door closed and turned to him. "Well?"

She almost laughed, because it was pretty clear he wanted to use the "long story" excuse again. Finally, he gestured to the dining room table. "Maybe we should talk while you eat your... What is that?"

"What, they don't have frozen macaroni and cheese in Heaven?"

"I have no idea. I've never been. But it seems to me that you can't call a place Heaven if it doesn't have pasta and cheese. And dogs."

"Agreed." She opened the silverware drawer. "But let me get this straight. Your dad is 'sort of' evil and you've never been to Heaven. What kind of angel *are* you, anyway?"

A nervous knot formed in her stomach as she palmed a fork. What if he *wasn't* an angel? What if he was lying? Oh, gods, who had she let into her house?

And how effective were forks as weapons? As one of Portland's most in-demand masseuses, she had a detailed knowledge of anatomy and could disable or even kill with one well-placed stab of a fork, but that was assuming the target was human. Even if Hawkyn wasn't an angel, he *definitely* wasn't human.

He must have noticed her alarm, because he lowered his voice to a soothing, almost lulling murmur. "I'm a special breed of earthbound angel called Memitim. I was born here, raised by humans, and my goal, same as every Memitim, is to earn my way into Heaven."

She raked him from head to toe with her gaze, looking for any sign that he was telling the truth, but he looked like a normal humanoid male. Well, not normal. Or in any way average. Hell, as far as she could tell, he didn't have a single physical attribute that wasn't utter perfection, from his flawless tan skin and angular, masculine features to his strong jawline and lush lashes that framed eyes the color of smoked emeralds.

Now she wanted to see all that perfection with his clothes off. After all, if he was really an angel, he'd be perfect in *every* way, right?

He probably wouldn't take kindly to her asking him to strip for proof, but surely he wouldn't object to a very basic demand he probably heard often.

"Let me see your wings."

A smear of pink brightened his cheeks. "Memitim don't have wings," he said, which sounded like a convenient excuse. "Not real ones. But I have something similar." Before she could ask what he meant, a pair of misty, smoke-colored wings punched into the air behind him. "These allow me to move invisibly when I need to."

Her mouth went dry with shock. He really was an angel. She was standing in the presence of a being she hadn't thought was real. Heck, she had always been *this close* to being an atheist, despite the existence of demons which, some would say, proved the existence of God.

"Can I touch them?"

"You can try." He shifted, allowing her access. "But your hand will pass through them. They're made of shadow."

She reached out, expecting to feel empty air, but instead her fingers felt...something. Something electric. He went taut as she stroked the apex of one of his ghostly wings.

"I can sense your touch," he breathed. "You can...feel them?"

"Yes," she said, in absolute awe that she was in contact with a real, Heavenly being. Well, an earthbound Heavenly being, anyway. "They feel like warm water with an electrical current running through it."

Curious, she concentrated on absorbing some of his energy through her palm, but nothing happened. She dropped her gaze to his perfect ass. Maybe if she touched a more solid part of his body...

"I don't understand." He stepped away, his expression one of genuine confusion. "No one has ever been able to touch them. This is the first time I've gotten any sensation from them at all."

Huh. Weird. "What did it feel like?"

"Like...a caress. Like they were real wings and they were connected to my—" He broke off and gave her a cheeky grin. "Never mind."

Too late. Her gaze slid downward, and she drew an appreciative breath at the impressive bulge behind the fly of his jeans.

So that was how you seduced an angel. Not that she planned to seduce him. She was an Earth girl, fond of the human realm and human people. Besides, she doubted angels fraternized with humans, let alone demons or human/demon hybrids like her.

Clearing her throat, she snapped her eyes back up to his face, but his amused expression said he knew she'd been ogling his angelic junk.

"So...other Memitim don't have shadow wings?" she asked, hoping she didn't sound too humiliated. "Why do you?"

"As I said, my father is evil. Less so now than when any of us were conceived, but back then, he was indistinguishable from a demon." He rotated his shoulders, and the wings melted away like smoke in a breeze. "He's a fallen angel, the father of all Memitim, so some of us inherit unique traits and abilities from him." He snorted. "Pisses off Heavenly-born angels that we get fallen angel skills they can't access."

"Wow," she whispered, trying to process this and failing. "How old are you?"

"A little over six hundred years old. Younger than most of my siblings. You?"

Six hundred years? Her people were long-lived, but not *that* long-lived, and their lifespans were only getting shorter as they bred more and more with humans.

"I'll be thirty next month," she said. "My parents are in their eighties, but they look my age."

She sat down at her vintage black and red table with her pasta, but she was no longer hungry. She'd grown up in a human environment, in a human neighborhood, attended human schools, and worked at human jobs. Her parents and brother were, for all intents and purposes, human. She and her family members embraced the powers they'd been born with, but she'd never really considered them to be supernatural. They were simply part of her. Like her hair and teeth.

So this...was unsettling. Hell, the events of the last few days, starting with being kidnapped and tortured, to waking up in a demon hospital, to sitting down at a table with an angel... All of it was messing with her head. It had, in fact, started to throb.

Bracing her elbows on the table, she rubbed her temples. "I...I think I need a minute."

"You okay? Aurora?" He appeared next to her, his hand on her shoulder. She hadn't even seen him move. "You're a little pale."

"I feel woozy." The room was starting to spin, and her stomach lurched like it wanted to empty itself of the nothingness inside. Shit, this was happening because she was out of power, wasn't it? She needed to recharge, and fast.

"I'm taking you back to Underworld General."

"I'd rather go to the police." Whoa. There were bright lights floating in front of her eyes now, and was she slurring her words? "Why can't I?"

"Aurora—"

"Tell me," she snapped, her patience worn down to a nubbin.

There was a slight hesitation, and then he said quietly, "You can't go to the police because Drayger is under protection."

The lights were starting to dim and darkness was closing in. "Whose protection?"

"Mine," he said slowly. "My job is to keep Drayger safe."

With those insane words, she welcomed the darkness.

Chapter Ten

Hawkyn caught Aurora as she slid out of the chair. Dammit, he shouldn't have dumped so much information on her so quickly. The doctors at Underworld General had assured him that she was physically fine, so she must be in shock, horrified as hell by his admission.

How could she not be? It was seriously fucked up that people like Drayger, the worst people to have ever lived, had been, and would continue to be, protected from harm while decent people suffered.

Tucking her against his chest, he carried her over to the couch, a retro velvet floral thing that didn't look like it could hold her petite frame, let alone his. He wondered why she favored '50s and '60s décor.

It was curious... He was hundreds of years old, and there was no single period in history that he looked back upon with fondness. Life sucked for humans for most of their history, and in some places, it still sucked. Really, he liked modern times, the technology, the entertainment, the food.

The females.

In modern times, females wore fewer clothes.

Even Aurora, in calf-length gray paisley leggings and a long V-neck teal sweater that complimented her creamy skin and bright blue eyes, was showing more of her curvy body than the women of his youth. And a good percentage of his adulthood, come to think about it.

In his arms, she started to stir, and he had to fight the sudden urge to hold her close instead of putting her down. She was the first female besides his sisters he'd held against his body in centuries. Even then, back when he'd thought he was human and before he was forced by Memitim rules into celibacy, contact with females had been purely sexual, quick fucks in alleyways and stables.

He'd been devastatingly poor, a thief when he couldn't scrounge enough work to feed himself, but he'd been handsome and charismatic, attracting females like a magnet. Those moments, as fleeting and seedy as they were, had been his only source of pleasure and his only escape from a life of misery.

"Sorry," she rasped as he set her gently on the sofa. "I think I used too much energy to power the protective ward around the house. I'll be okay in a minute." She shifted so she was sitting up, braced on the armrest, legs tucked beneath her. She was too pale, her eyes bloodshot, but she radiated an inner strength Hawkyn could feel like an electric current on the surface of his skin. "Did you really say that the bastard who tortured me and wants me dead is under your protection?"

There was no way to sugarcoat his answer. "Yes. He's what we call Primori, and I have a duty to keep him safe."

"Okay," she said, a lot more calmly than he would have if the situation had been reversed. "Let's come back to why an angel would be protecting a serial killer and focus on why that means I can't go to the police."

There was no way to sugarcoat this, either. All he had was a bunch of bitter pills to swallow. He could at least offer her some water to take them with.

"You can't go to the police because I fucked up." He sank down in the surprisingly comfortable aqua chair that matched precisely nothing in the house. "I interfered in the parking lot and you blasted me instead of him, potentially changing his fate."

Her skeptical expression would have made him laugh if they'd been talking about anything other than a psychopath bent on butchering her.

"Um, correct me if I'm wrong, but doesn't that mean that I would have killed him? So what's the big deal about going to the police? Or, you know, killing him?"

"We don't know that you would have killed him," he explained. "It's possible you would have missed. Or only injured him." It was also possible that Atticus was wrong and Drayger wasn't entirely human or that he was protected by an enchanted object or a mystical spell. "You could still have ended up being abducted."

"Then why did you rescue me?"

Because apparently he was good at compounding mistakes. "Because I didn't want to take the chance that you weren't supposed to be abducted."

She sat up a little straighter, eyes flaring the way Suzanne's did when she was about to lay into him, and he braced himself. "So you're telling me that if you hadn't been there but you knew he'd taken me, you *wouldn't* have rescued me?"

"Memitim can't interfere with the actions of those we watch over."

"You asshole!" Color flooded her cheeks and her gorgeous eyes flashed angry fire. "You would have just watched me be slowly taken apart?"

"Well, I wouldn't have *watched...*"

"Get out!" She picked up the bright red vase from the end table and hurled it at him, just like something out of a movie. He ducked as it whooshed past his ear and shattered against the wall. "Get out of my house!"

Clearly she needed some time to absorb all of this. Unfortunately, she also needed to be safe. "I'm not going anywhere until you put up the protection spell again."

He'd be sure to cast a protective ward on the house as well, but he wouldn't leave her for long. Wards weren't his specialty and they tended to wear off quickly.

Jaw still clenched with anger, she averted her gaze, taking sudden interest in the coffee table. "I can't."

"Why not?"

"Because my power is drained," she ground out. "I don't have enough to light a candle, let alone weave a complex protection spell."

"How do you recharge?" At her hesitation, he leaned back in the chair, hoping to appear less threatening, the way kind people had done to him during his childhood. He'd never forget how small gestures—a smile, a crumb of food, or merely a little patience had helped him survive. To be powerless was bad enough, but having to explain your vulnerability only made it worse. "It's okay. I get it. I have to recharge too."

She glanced over at him, the wariness in her gaze dimming slightly. "You do?"

He nodded. "It's another one of those inherited things from my father. Some of us, like my sister Suzanne, don't experience a complete drain on their powers. But most of us do."

This time when she looked over at him, she didn't look away. "And how do *you* restore your energy?"

"Sleep or time. Or..." He opened his mouth to reveal his fangs. "We feed."

"Oh." Her eyes flared in surprise, but darkened as she looked at him. "*Oh.*"

He already knew she was special somehow, given that she could feel his shadow wings, but now her sultry voice flowed through him like hot honey, slow and sweet, and his body responded, awakening from a centuries-long coma. The thaw had started when he'd sensed her fleeting touch on his wings, but this was even more intense. He felt a little logy but at the same time euphoric, as if he'd shotgunned a barrel of Champagne.

This was bad. He'd spent dozens of years teaching himself to suppress his carnal desires—at least, the ones that involved him and a partner. Memitim were supposed to avoid self-gratification as well, but masturbation had fallen into a "don't ask, don't tell" thing over the last few decades, and he'd never really obeyed anyway.

Now he was getting all kinds of feedback from the body he'd always considered perfectly trained and conditioned, mentally, emotionally, and physically.

This was exactly why Memitim weren't supposed to interact much outside of the Memitim community. This was exactly what he lectured Suzanne about.

And this was exactly what could get him eliminated from consideration to be appointed to the Memitim Council.

"Who...who do you feed from?" Aurora asked, her curiosity overriding her residual anger.

"Whoever we want, really." His mouth started to water just thinking about it. "My brother Maddox can only restore his power by drinking from demons. Some of my siblings prefer feeding from their Primori, but I've always preferred to feed from people who prey on others."

She shuddered, but when she spoke, her voice was steady. "Is their blood stronger? Better fuel or something?"

Her theory made sense, given that Primori were all special in some way, and human predators were a special kind of scumbag, but no, that wasn't why he did it.

"I feed from people who hurt others because it forces them to feel the pain and helplessness they inflict on their victims." When Memitim fed, they were supposed to do it while their donors were sleeping, but that was one of the other guidelines he chose to ignore. "We can feed without causing pain... We can even make it pleasurable. But some people don't deserve that."

"A friend of mine claimed she was bitten by a vampire once." Aurora's slim fingers stroked her throat absently, as if imagining a set of shiny fangs buried deep. "She said it was amazing."

He'd never understood the fascination with vampires, nor the erotic nature of feeding, but the idea of latching onto Aurora's vein and taking her inside him for nourishment was suddenly his number one fantasy.

Shut it down, man. She just went through a traumatic experience.

"I'll take her word for it," he said, but damn, now he couldn't get the idea out of his head. "Now, what about you? How do you recharge?"

For a long, drawn-out moment, she eyed him, probably trying to decide if she should tell him. And then, just as she opened her mouth, Drayger's *heraldi* sparked to life, vibrating with a proximity alert.

"Shit." He shoved to his feet and raced over to the window. There was no one in sight, not even a passerby with a dog. But he could feel a dark presence. And it was close. Drayger had brought his evil side out to play.

"What is it?"

"Not what. Who."

"Drayger." She leaped to her feet and shoved them into the black flats under the coffee table. "Where?"

"I don't know, but we need to get out of here." He took her hand and flashed to Sheoul-gra...

Except he didn't. They were still standing in her living room.

She looked up at him. "Is this the part where you do something to get us out of here?"

"I was pausing for effect." He tried again. Nothing. Fuck.

"I get it," she said, releasing his hand to peek through a crack in the curtains. "You're a drama queen. Can we go now?"

"I can't flash. Your trap must have drained me." He dug into his pocket for his cell phone. Cipher or one of his siblings would come for them. But the moment he saw the scorch marks streaking his phone's plastic and metal casing, his heart sank. "Your trap fried my powers *and* my phone. Can I use yours?"

She moved toward a yellow table where a charger sat, but she stopped after two steps and cursed. "It was in my purse. Drayger got it."

He didn't miss the slight waver in her voice when she'd spoken Drayger's name. "Where's your landline?"

"I don't have one." She scowled. "Do people even have those anymore?"

Son of a bitch. "Computer?"

"My laptop was in my car. Which has probably been towed by now." She hugged herself as if cold, her gaze darting from window to window. All her curtains were drawn and her back door locked, but the open floor plan left them too exposed. "Look, Drayger is just a human. We can walk out. He can't hurt you, right?"

"Most likely, no." He guided her toward her bedroom, which was a green and orange '50s bonanza. "Pack a bag. We'll get out of here and find a Harrowgate. You can use it to get us to Sheoul-gra."

She frowned up at him. "What's Sheoul-gra?"

He stared at her in disbelief. "How can you not know that? You're a demon."

"This isn't the time for a lesson in all things Wytch," she snapped as she hurried toward the bedroom closet, "but I assure you, I'm not a demon. Most of us have so much human DNA in us that we have only a fraction of the powers our ancestors had. Our people are dying out because we tend to mate with humans and dilute the Wytch genes." As he eased up to the window to look out, she whipped a duffel bag from the closet and started filling it. "But there's now a growing movement to save our people, like the Wytch dating websites."

"Online Wytch dating? Have you tried it?"

"Ugh." She disappeared into the tiny bathroom, where she banged around in drawers and cupboards as she talked. "Sort of. My mom signed me up. I've never gone on a date, though. I don't feel the need to date other Wytches just to preserve our race. Man, that pisses off the parents and every old-school Wytch on the planet." She emerged with a toiletry bag, which she tossed into the duffel before zipping it. Straightening, she squared her shoulders and faced him, her gaze fierce and unafraid, her jaw set in a stubborn line. "I'm ready."

No, he feared she wasn't ready. If she didn't know what Sheoulgra was, there was no way she was ready for what she was about to see.

* * * *

There was a serial killer outside Aurora's house, a serial killer determined to butcher her slowly, and yet she was perfectly calm. Well, "calm" was a bit of an exaggeration, given that she was shaking like a leaf and her heart was tap dancing on her rib cage. But the fact that she wasn't alone, and that the person with her was an angel, gave her a much-needed boost of confidence that she wasn't going to die.

Of course, the fact that said angel might let her die if "fate" required it was a little disconcerting.

"Front door or back?" she asked.

Hawkyn heaved her duffel over his shoulder, the ropey muscles in his arm flexing with every fluid motion. "Front." He moved to the living room. "Stay next to me. I won't let anything happen to you."

He took her hand and opened the front door slowly, peering out before giving the signal to go. But as they passed over the threshold, she struck an invisible force. Pain radiated through her nose and cheekbones as she bounced back into the house.

Instantly, Hawkyn rushed back inside. "Aurora!" He dropped the duffel and framed her face in his hands, his sharp gaze assessing her for injuries. "What happened? Are you okay?"

She nodded, cupping her nose. "I felt a ward. The bastard trapped me inside here."

A blast of heat roared through the house, and the temperature shot up at least twenty degrees. She always kept the house at sixty-five degrees this time of year, so the instant jump to summer temps was like stepping into a dry sauna.

"How the fuck is he doing this?" Hawkyn's raw curse bounced off the walls. "He's going to force heat exhaustion and then take you while you're too weak to fight back. We need to get you out of here *now*." He slid one warm hand down, his fingers skimming lightly over her jaw and lower, to the sensitive skin on her neck. His gaze darkened, locking with hers. "With your permission."

Blinking, momentarily confused, she watched him flick the pink tip of his tongue across a fang. Oh, right. He could feed from her to recharge. Take her blood with those huge, gleaming canines.

She waited for the revulsion to kick in, but instead, something else happened. Something...hot. Hotter than the serial-killer induced heat that was testing the limits of her deodorant, building quickly, as if they were inside a pre-heating oven. Her breasts became achy, and between her legs, a honeyed rush of wetness bloomed.

There's a serial killer outside.

The sudden thought came with a blast of memories, of Drayger with the scalpel that made tiny, stinging cuts. Of him with the skinning knife that removed flesh with a wet sound you could hear through your screams. Sharp things and his laughter and pain—

"Will it hurt?" she blurted.

"I'll make it feel good, I promise." A fresh blast of heat drove up the number on the thermostat near the door to 103. "But we need to hurry."

She nodded, and his emerald eyes darkened even more, holding her gaze prisoner as he lowered his head toward hers. Gently, he tilted her face to the side and opened his mouth over her throat, and she shuddered with a mix of anticipation and trepidation. She'd only dated a handful of men in her thirty years, wasting most of them on her high school sweetheart, a human who had never known the truth about her. If he had, he might not have cheated on her during their junior year in college. Then again, maybe he enjoyed the curse of flatulence she'd cast upon him, affecting him every time he kissed a girl.

The other guys had come after the breakup, nothing serious, mostly rebound dates she'd used for sex. Wytches needed to discharge their energy often, either with sex or magic, and she'd gone through an extended anti-magic phase for a while. But not one of those sexual partners had made her nervous the way Hawkyn did.

Granted, none of them had fangs. Nor had they been supernatural beings, let alone angels. And none of them had looked like Hawkyn, with his six and a half foot, thickly-muscled build, a cocky smile that radiated confidence, and intelligent eyes that she doubted missed anything.

Hawkyn's breath whispered over her skin, and she shivered as her anxiety became excitement. As his tongue flicked across her vein, she even had to hold back a moan of pleasure. When his fangs sank into her flesh, the mild pinprick gave way to a shocking spear of ecstasy that went straight to her core.

His arm slipped around her, bracing her body against his big one as he disengaged his teeth and repositioned his mouth. She let herself go, let herself sink into him as he swept her up and then settled them both on the couch so she was straddling his lap, her sex pressed firmly against the impressive arousal behind the fly of his jeans.

He took slow, easy draws, one hand holding her head in place, the other gripping her waist, settled tamely above her hipbone. His pinky finger wedged between her waistband and her sweater, and consciously or subconsciously he was stroking skin, his touch adding to the heat that was building inside and out.

Under the circumstances, was it bad that she wanted to rock against him to ease the maddening desire? But despite his erection, he made no indication that he wanted anything more than her blood, and she sensed he'd chosen this position not because of how they fit together, but because he could keep an eye on both entrances and most of the windows.

A drop of sweat trickled down her temple, and she glanced at the thermometer. 115 now.

Shifting slightly, Hawkyn let out a groan and swept his tongue over the punctures in her throat. She felt no pain, only a pinch and tingle that told her the holes were sealing themselves.

"Are we done?" she whispered, making no move to climb off him. She wasn't even sure she could. Her bones felt like noodles and her muscles like water.

She was still ragingly horny, though. So horny she'd forgotten to make an attempt at drawing energy from him, even though her palms had been pressed against his back, holding him close as he took long, deep pulls from her vein.

"Yeah," he said roughly, tucking her head into the crook of his neck and shoulder. "I just need a minute to clear the fog."

"The fog? Outside?"

His chuckle made her bounce, and she almost gasped at the electric sensation of her breasts rubbing against his chest.

"In my head." He arched, just a little, and she *did* gasp at how his erection rocked into her mound. "And my body."

"I get that," she murmured into his shoulder. "Because I feel like I drank a couple of Long Island Ice Teas spiked with some kind of super-aphrodisiac." Reluctantly, she pushed herself up, just in time for another heatwave.

125.

"Come on," he said, lifting her off him. "We're going someplace much cooler."

"And where's that?"

He grinned as he flipped the duffel into the air with his foot and caught it in his hand in one easy motion. "Hell," he said, taking her hand. "We're going to Hell."

Chapter Eleven

Aurora didn't have a chance to ask Hawkyn what he meant by saying they were going to Hell. One moment they were baking like oatmeal raisin cookies in her house, and the next they were standing on some sort of raised platform in a place that resembled part of an ancient Greek city.

She looked down at the round stone pad beneath their feet. "How did you do this?"

"Angels can flash directly to or from this portal. Almost everyone else arrives via a twin portal in the human realm."

Okay, but where, exactly, were they? Lush, green grounds stretched forever, dotted by fountains and forests, streams and paths. A massive white building with doors that could allow entrance to a dinosaur was flanked by smaller buildings, temples, and courtyards where people sparred or practiced with weapons, and seated in a small amphitheater nearby, what appeared to be a handful of bored-looking students were listening to a robed guy giving a lecture.

"This...this is Hell?"

"Sort of."

How could someplace be "sort of" Hell? Was it like how his father was "sort of" evil?

Hawkyn squeezed her hand, pressing his palm against hers in just the right spot, and a current of energy sizzled up her arm, astonishing in its intensity and made even more astonishing by the fact that she could feel it spilling into the empty tank inside her that held her power. Usually she had to make an effort to absorb energy from people, and it was a slow, steady charge; it never rushed in like water from a broken dam.

When he released her hand, her knees wobbled from the sudden disconnection from his nuclear-grade fuel. He gave her a brief once-over that wasn't remotely sexual, but tingles followed wherever his gaze landed.

"You okay?" he asked.

No. Not at all. Touching an angel running on a full battery took some getting used to.

"I'm fine. Just a little freaked out about being in Hell, you know?" *Holy shit.* "This isn't exactly what I expected."

"That's because this probably isn't what you think it is." He nodded in the direction of a marble statue of two horned, hooved demons fighting with a trident and a spear. "The demon realm is called Sheoul—it's what most people think of when they reference Hell. But Sheoul isn't where evil human souls go." He made an encompassing gesture with his hand. "This is Sheoul-gra, sort of a sub-realm that houses the true Hell, where the souls of demons and evil humans are kept until they're reincarnated."

She looked around, but it was hard to believe this place was full of malevolent souls. "I don't understand. Where are the souls?"

He guided her down a stone path toward a blocky building with a lot of glass-less windows. "They're kept in the Inner Sanctum."

"I see," she said, even though she didn't. "So why are we here?"

"It's where I live."

She nearly tripped over her own feet. Angels lived in Hell? Since when? *What was happening?* Somehow she managed to not blurt any of that out, instead keeping her cool the way her brother had always taught her and asking just one tame question. There would be others later. Many others.

"Why?" she asked. "Angels living in Hell is contrary to everything I was ever taught."

Not that she'd gone to church or anything, but seeing how religion was everywhere, she'd managed to pick up a few things, and one constant in all the various religions that mentioned angels was that they resided in the other, less demon-y place.

As they walked through a grassy courtyard, he explained how Memitim were raised by humans, taken from the human world as young adults, and trained at various locations around the world, but that they could also come here to live and train...because apparently, their father, the father of all Memitim, ruled this realm.

As they approached a building Hawkyn called Hotel Hell, panic frayed the edges of her control. She was in a strange place full of strange beings, and she didn't know nearly enough to be comfortable here in the least. She needed more information before she went any further.

Planting her feet, she grabbed his arm and pulled him to a stop. "Wait. I need more."

He gazed down at her, his brow furrowed. "More what?"

"Information."

"Such as?"

A bird flew by, a bird that looked a lot like a robin. But hey, sure, if there were angels living in Hell, why not robins?

Aurora looked around, wondering if all the people milling about were his brothers and sisters. "You said your father rules this realm? Who is he?"

Please don't say Satan. Please don't say Satan. Please don't say Satan.

"His name is Azagoth," he said, and she nearly giggled at how foolish she'd been to think, even for a measly second, that a legendary being as evil as Satan could father angels. "You probably know him as the Grim Reaper."

Her knees went wobbly again, but for a very different reason. She stumbled, but in a blur of motion, Hawkyn caught her, steadying her against his hard body.

"I'm sorry," he murmured. "I took too much blood."

"No," she said quickly. "No. This is just a lot to take in. I mean, forty-eight hours ago I wasn't even sure God was real, and now I'm in...in...Hell. With the Grim Reaper."

"I get it." He nodded in sympathy. "I thought I was human until one of my Memitim brothers plucked me out of a bad situation and dropped me inside a Belgian castle full of fellow angels."

"And how did *you* take it when your world was turned upside down?"

Winking, he gave her a panty-melter of a grin. "I passed out cold."

She laughed, doubting it was true but appreciating that he was trying to make her comfortable in a freaky situation. But the reality caught up with her again when one of the demons in the statue she'd seen a few minutes ago moved, curling its lips and revealing another row of sharp six-inch teeth.

"Thank you for getting me away from Drayger," she said, keeping one eye on the creepy statue, "but I can't stay here indefinitely. I can stay at a hotel in Portland or in one of the guest rooms at the spa where I work." Her boss, Jenna, was always letting employees stay when they needed to, so it most likely wouldn't be a problem. Just an inconvenience.

"No, you can't." He waved at a group of people talking around a picnic table. So normal. So *weird*. "Drayger is dangerous. He can somehow track his victims anywhere in the world in hours, and until we find out how, you can't be anywhere he can easily get to you."

"This is bullshit." He'd started moving again, but she refused to budge. None of this made sense, and if her life was going to be upended, she wanted to know why. "I shouldn't have to run from someone who should be in jail, and who *would* be in jail if I went to the police. And you still haven't explained why you're protecting the bastard."

He opened his mouth, and she could see it in his face. He was going to spew more "It's a long story" BS. No. Just no.

She jammed a finger into his sternum and got right up in his face. On her tiptoes. Later she'd probably be horrified by her audacity in going toe to toe with an angel, but in this moment, for her own sanity, she needed to be in charge.

"I want to know what the deal is." She poked hard. "Now."

"You're right." Reaching up, he engulfed her hand in his. He didn't push her away. He just looked at her, almost with amusement. "I wasn't going to do this, but come on."

He wheeled around and, keeping hold of her hand, which she angled so he wouldn't touch the spot near her index finger that would trigger a download of his nuclear-grade energy, he led her through a side door of the massive Greek manor. Once inside, he guided her through a shiny, modern kitchen that could have belonged to an upscale restaurant.

"This kitchen serves my father and his mate, and all his senior staff. There are more kitchens in the dorm buildings that serve Memitim and Unfallen."

"Unfallen?"

"Fallen angels who haven't entered Sheoul," he explained. "When an angel loses his wings, he or she is dropped into the Earthly realm and has two choices. They can enter Sheoul and complete their fall from grace in trade for evil powers, or they can remain powerless and disgraced, but still have a chance of redeeming themselves." He pushed open a door and they stepped into an elegant dining hall, its walls covered in tapestries and art depicting scenes from eras all over the world. And underworld. "They live here because it's safe."

"What do Unfallen angels have to fear?"

"Everything. Since they lose their angelic powers and don't have fallen angel powers either, they're weak. Heavenly angels will kill them, and fallen angels will drag them against their will into Sheoul, which turns them evil. Demons have little use for them, either, and they score a lot of bragging points by being able to say they killed an angel, even if they're just Unfallen." He glanced at his watch. "We should still have time..."

"Time for what? You were supposed to be telling me why you're protecting Drayger."

He knocked on another door. "I'm enlisting help to do that."

The door swung open, revealing a smaller room, cozy, with a couple of sofas, overstuffed chairs, and a coffee table all arranged in a circle. As they walked inside, two women looked up from the papers and colored markers scattered on the tabletop.

"Hey, bro." One of them gave a little wave and tucked a lock of dark curls behind her ear. "Lilliana and I were just planning next week's menu. Any requests?"

"Yeah. How about that New York strip steak you make? The one with the feta and caramelized onions." He grinned at Aurora. "It's awesome." His palm pressed lightly on her back. "Suzanne, Lilliana, this is Aurora. I have to summon someone from the embassy, and I was hoping that while I'm doing that you could fill her in on...well...this." He made a gesture that she figured encompassed all the weirdness.

Lilliana seemed to understand, because she looked both amused and sympathetic. "Of course. But I'm going to need some context."

Hawkyn hesitated, and Aurora started to sweat a little. Then she sweated a lot when he finally said, "I don't want any lectures about how I fucked up."

Clapping with delight, Suzanne sat up straight, an impish smile on her slightly rounded face. "Ooh, my perfect big brother messed up. What stupid thing did you do that I get to hold over your head?"

He jerked his thumb at Aurora. "I saved her life."

"And he still hasn't explained why that's a bad thing," Aurora muttered.

Hawkyn sighed. "One of my Primori was going to kill her, and I saved her."

Suzanne's eyes flared with surprise while Lilliana patted the cushion next to her. "Come have a seat, Aurora. We'll get you a cup of tea and something to eat, and then we'll explain everything."

"Thank you, Lilliana." Hawkyn glanced over at Suzanne. "I don't know how long I'll be. Will you make sure Aurora is settled into a guest room?"

"Did you clear it with Cat?"

He gave her a sheepish grin. "I was hoping you'd do that too."

"Don't try Cipher's charm tricks on me," Suzanne said with a wag of her finger. "They don't work."

"So that's a yes?" At Suzanne's annoyed huff, Hawkyn's grin turned victorious. "Thanks, sis." He turned to Aurora. "You can ask these two anything you want. They'll be straight with you, and you can trust them. I'll see you soon."

He took off before she could figure out how she felt about being left in a strange Hell dimension with two strangers, but ultimately, it was better than being back in Drayger's cargo container.

She hoped.

* * * *

Hawkyn sent a summons to both the Memitim Council and the embassy, figuring either could help him out. Whoever they sent as representatives would be pissed to know he'd sent a double summons, but at this point, he didn't give a shit. He needed answers.

He paced like a lion in a cage as he waited, his patience in tatters as the clock ticked off the hour mark. Finally, just as he was about to send another set of summons, an Ascended brother he didn't know materialized at the Summoning Stone, his dark skin and hair glowing even after the light beam that accompanied his arrival faded.

"I am Demetrius, Ninth Chief of Embassy Operations, son of Azagoth and Luscindia. What is your request, Hawkyn, son of Azagoth and Ulnara?"

First, he wanted Demetrius to lay off the formality. Hawkyn would take Jacob's "What do you want, asshole?" over an overstuffed, pompous douchebag with too much starch in his holy robes.

But he probably shouldn't say that.

"Hey, bro," he drawled, countering his half-brother's formality. "I need to speak to Atticus, keeper of bizarrely detailed notes, son of Azagoth and...some angel."

"You know the rules. Earthbound Memitim aren't supposed to be in contact with Ascended Memitim unless they're employed by the Council or the embassy. Which he is not."

"Yes, I know," Hawkyn ground out. "But this is a special circumstance."

"Aren't they all?"

Hawkyn gnashed his teeth in frustration. "It's a stupid rule, and it needs to be changed. Who do I see about that?"

"You can bring it up with a Council member."

"You mean the Council members who never respond to our summons? How can I bring it up to them if I can't talk to them?"

Demetrius's eyes, so brown they were almost black, took in the surroundings with interest, even though his monotone voice couldn't sound any more bored. "Then contact the embassy."

"I just did. You told me to contact the Council."

"That's because they make the rules," Demetrius explained slowly, as if he were speaking to Idess's toddler, even though he was the one with the idiotic circular argument that made no sense. Hawkyn wanted to scream.

"How about you deliver my message?"

"Not my job."

Hawkyn hated this guy. "Look, I just need a minute with Atticus. We're told to protect our Primori and their fates at all costs, right? Well, to protect mine, I need to know more about him, and maybe Atticus can fill in some blanks."

"Hawkyn, this is your second inquiry about the same Primori in just days." Demetrius crossed his arms over his chest. "Why? Are you in trouble?"

Hawkyn barked out a bitter laugh. "Do you honestly think I'd tell you? The system doesn't exactly encourage coming forward, not when we're punished for doing so."

"That's the way it's always been."

"That doesn't mean it's the best way." And it was exactly why he wanted to join the Council after he Ascended. Shit needed to be changed. The Old Guard needed to be replaced.

In many ways, the earthly realm progressed faster than the demon and Heavenly ones, simply because the short human lifespan meant that there were frequent turnovers of ideas and practices. When a species was immortal, ancient customs persisted in the minds and hearts of ancient beings—ancient beings who were always the ones running the shows. They resisted new things in favor of the old ways, even if the old ways no longer worked in modern ages.

Yes, the Council was in dire need of fresh blood.

Demetrius huffed and rolled his eyes. "If you have nothing other than a request I'm not going to grant, I'll be going now." He sneered at something over Hawkyn's shoulder. "This place is claustrophobic."

It absolutely was, but there was no way Hawkyn was going to admit that to Demetrius.

"Really? I hadn't noticed." He moved to block his half-brother's path to the Summoning Stone. "There's one more thing. I want to know if Jason Drayger's Fate Line has been altered."

Demetrius' dark brow punched down in an angry V. "Are you planning to cold-cock me like you did Jacob?"

"Depends on how much you piss me off." Hawkyn's hand clenched as if it had a mind of its own and remembered the feel of crunching into Jacob's perfect nose. "Come on. Just...give me this. Remember when you were earthbound, worried about your Primori? Imagine how much more effective you could have been if you'd known whether or not your charges were on the right course. We should all have access to that information, don't you think?"

"It doesn't matter what I think," Demetrius said, his tone softer than it had been before. Even his expression had lost its etched-in-stone seriousness as his gaze turned inward. "This is the way things have always been done. But..." Demetrius looked around and, apparently satisfied that no one was within hearing distance, he turned back to Hawkyn. "No, your Primori's Fate Line is intact. I checked on it before I came."

Shock filtered its way through Hawkyn's system. It was good news, but baffling. He'd truly thought that his interference in Aurora's abduction had changed the future. Apparently not. So had Aurora been fated to be captured but escape even without Hawkyn's help? Or would she simply have escaped without seriously injuring Drayger in the parking lot if he hadn't been there?

And what did they do now?

Chapter Twelve

Aurora was in awe of everything around her, including Lilliana and Suzanne. Suzanne was so...normal. She was upbeat, friendly, and had a passion for cooking and fashion magazines. Lilliana, an angel born and raised in Heaven, was smart, thoughtful, and mated to the Grim Reaper himself.

At that particular revelation, Aurora had choked on the tea and cinnamon scones Suzanne had brought her. And, for the record, the scones were incredible. Hawkyn's sister had even been nice enough to put a couple in a box along with other homemade pastries for Aurora to take to the Hotel Hell room Suzanne had set her up with.

The room was simple and small, more like a college dorm than a hotel room. There was a single bed, a small desk, and a tiny bathroom, but the TV was nice and there was even a computer, on which she'd spent the last half hour while she waited for Hawkyn.

The revelation that Drayger could track her had stuck with her, engaging her curiosity as much as it terrified her. She was a Wytch, and, while she liked to pretend she was basically human, she wasn't. She had powers and skills she couldn't deny, and when a supernatural force was used against her, her instinct to fight back roared to the surface. If Drayger was using a spell to find her, surely she could use one to counter it.

She just had to find one.

Fortunately, in a private, secure corner of the Internet, Wytches gathered to share tips, tricks, and instructions for performing various tasks such as protecting one's self from psychos who could find you after tasting your blood. And according to a user named

Wytches_Float, all she needed to do was taste *Drayger's* blood while having sex.

Hard pass on that one.

Another user, HocusPocus, claimed that turning a drop of Drayger's blood into iron would render him unable to use his tracking ability. Naturally, he didn't include instructions on how to perform such a feat. Not that she had a way of collecting Drayger's blood. And really, if she could get his blood, why wouldn't she just kill him?

Probably because Hawkyn was protecting the bastard.

Lilliana and Suzanne had explained the reason, which made sense in a lot of ways, but none of them made her feel any better.

"Most of the people we protect are decent folks," Suzanne had said. "But unfortunately, evil people sometimes play a role in the advancement of humanity. Change often comes from tragedy or from evil, even if it isn't obvious at the time."

"Really?" Aurora had asked, her skepticism flag flying high. "Such as?"

"Wars are responsible for a lot of medical, industrial, and technological advancements," she'd said.

"And," Lilliana had added, "sometimes the good that comes from evil doesn't happen on a large scale. An evil person or an evil act can effect change in laws or individuals, individuals who will then go on to do great things. Or maybe even just make a difference in their own lives and those around them. We don't have to like evil, but there *is* a place for it. Trust that there's a plan. Someday, you'll see."

"Have you seen it? This plan?" Aurora asked, and a light had suddenly shone in Lilliana's eyes, an ethereal glow that had captivated her, surrounded her in a blanket of Heavenly warmth.

"I have. I don't know the future, but I do know that what seems random is not. Everything, from a rude remark a customer makes to a waiter, to a plane crash happens for a reason."

Great. But Aurora wasn't going to hold her breath waiting for the reason for her abduction to become clear. Nor was she going to sit around and let Drayger get hold of her again, no matter how important to humanity's future her death might be.

A tap on the door startled her, and thinking it was Hawkyn, she opened it eagerly. But instead, there was a pretty red-haired female standing there with a clipboard and a small basket full of toiletries.

"Hi," she said brightly. "I'm Cataclysm, but you can call me Cat. I'm in charge of guest housing and hospitality." She handed Aurora the basket. "A lot of people who stay here come unprepared, so I put together some items you might need."

This is so weird.

When Cat nodded, Aurora realized she'd spoken out loud. "Are you new to the supernatural world or Sheoul-gra?"

"Ah, kinda both."

Cat grinned. "Well, if it helps, people here are pretty cool. There are some douchewads, and some of the statues bite if you get too close, but for the most part, Sheoul-gra doesn't suck. Who are you here with?"

"Hawkyn," she said. "But I'm not *with* him. I mean, he brought me here, but we aren't together. Not like that..." Ugh. She was babbling like a lunatic. Time to move on, the way she did after she'd massaged all the tension out of one part of a customer's body. She'd certainly massaged this subject to death. "So, are you one of his sisters?"

"Nah." Cat tucked her clipboard under one arm. "I'm a fallen angel. I live in the Inner Sanctum with my mate."

"The Inner Sanctum... That's where the souls are kept, right? You live there?"

"Well, my mate, Hades, runs the place—"

"Wait." Aurora held up her hand. "What? Did you say *Hades*?"

Cat's grin was pure *ate-the-canary* satisfied. "Yep. *That* Hades. He's the Jailor of Souls, so he pretty much has to live in the jail. It's not my dream home, but you do what you have to do to be with the one you love, right?"

This place just kept getting weirder and weirder.

"Right," Aurora said, although she really couldn't see herself living someplace like this for anyone.

Hawkyn's image flashed in her head, which was insane, given that she'd only known him for a matter of hours. And she was *not* here *with* him.

Cat cocked her head and studied Aurora with such intensity that she had to force herself to not squirm. "I'm just curious—and you don't have to answer—but how do you know Hawkyn? Are you one of his Primori?"

Aurora shook her head. "He's protecting me from his Primori. And he might be protecting his Primori from me, as well."

For some reason, Cat's expression became troubled. "I see. Well, I'd better go—"

"Wait." Careful to avoid hitting the spot on her palm that might trigger a flow of energy, Aurora grabbed Cat's forearm as she turned to leave. "What's the matter?"

"It's nothing." Cat smiled reassuringly. "Really."

Aurora sighed. "Please don't bullshit me. I've had a really rough couple of days."

There was a moment of tense silence, and then Cat stepped closer and lowered her voice. "I love the people here. I admire the work Memitim do, because I know I couldn't do it. They're dedicated, passionate, and tough as nails." She hesitated, rolling her bottom lip between her teeth, and Aurora struggled to contain her impatience. Finally, Cat blurted, "But they can also be ruthless in their missions to protect their Primori. They'll do whatever it takes, even if their Primori is a genocidal maniac."

Aurora knew that. But for the first time, she was truly becoming aware of what that meant. "You're saying that if Hawkyn's Primori needs to kill me to fulfill his destiny or whatever—"

"Hawkyn will deliver you to him like a pizza."

* * * *

"Hey, brother." Emerico stopped near where Hawkyn was sitting on a park bench with Atticus's notes about Drayger. "Have you figured out what you're going to do about your serial killer predicament?"

Nope. And it was driving him nuts. He always had all the answers, and for the first time in longer than he could remember, he was at a loss.

"The only thing I can do right now is keep Aurora safe," he said, peering down at the notes that had begun to blur with uselessness.

"You know you can't keep her here, right?"

Hawk's gaze cut sharply to his brother. "As long as the Council and embassy don't know she's here, who cares?"

"Our father cares."

Alarm clanged inside him. "He knows?"

Hawkyn had figured Azagoth would find out sooner rather than later, given that Lilliana had met Aurora, but geez, it had only been a couple of hours. And Hawkyn didn't think he'd give a shit anyway. Azagoth didn't exactly follow the rules.

"I just spoke with him," Rico said. "I guess he saw Suzanne escorting her to Hotel Hell."

"Yeah, well, Memitim business isn't his business. What's it matter to him if I have her here?"

Rico shrugged. "I think he's trying to toe the Heavenly line." He rolled his eyes. "You know, for the first time ever. He wants something from them. Whatever it is, he wants it bad if he's playing their games."

Shit. This was unexpected. "Guess I'd better see him and get this cleared."

Another roll of Rico's dark eyes. "He'll probably let it slide. He lets his favorites get away with murder."

Hawkyn gaped. "You think I'm one of his favorites?"

"Lilliana likes you, so he likes you."

Ah, yes. Hawk had forgotten that there was no love lost between Lilliana and Rico. Hawkyn had no idea what Lilliana's side of the story was, but Rico had despised her since the day he claimed she'd slapped him for giving her a compliment. Hawkyn had known Rico for several decades longer than he'd known Lilliana...which was why he was almost certain Rico had deserved anything Lilliana did to him. He loved his brother, but the guy refused to take responsibility for his actions and always claimed he was the victim in any situation.

"Do you think he should let it slide?" Hawkyn asked, and Rico shrugged.

"I think her being here can only hurt you." Rico signaled to one of their sisters, who was tapping her foot impatiently at the tennis court. "Eva and I are practicing for the tennis tourney next week. You gonna root for us?"

"Sure," Hawkyn said absently. "See you later."

Rico took off and Hawkyn went straight to Azagoth's office. Zhubaal, his fallen angel assistant, granted him immediate entry. Inside, his father was observing a parade of demon souls escorted by his *griminions* as they guided the demons to their final destination in the Inner Sanctum. With the exception of one unfortunate accident, not a single soul got into the Sanctum without Azagoth's approval, and while most spent no more than a few seconds with the Grim Reaper, every once in a while he pulled one aside, and *no one* wanted to be *that* guy.

"Hawkyn." Azagoth didn't even turn to look at him. "Are you here to tackle me again?"

"Twice in twenty-four hours would be considered rude," Hawkyn said, mirroring the amused tone in his father's voice. It was always smart to start off any conversation with Azagoth on a positive note.

Azagoth grunted, which Hawk was going to take as a laugh. "Then what can I do for you?"

"I just talked to Emerico. He says you agree with him that Aurora should leave."

With a wave of his hand, Azagoth froze the soul parade in their tracks and turned to Hawkyn. "That's a slight mischaracterization of what I said."

Hope zinged through him. "Then she can stay?"

"No. I said I think you *should* be able to have her here." The fireplace on the far wall flared to life, sparked by nothing more than Azagoth's thoughts. "But there are rules. She has to go."

Son of a bitch. Hawk's heart sank to his feet. So much for hope. Aurora deserved better than this, and he was going to keep fighting for her. And this wasn't even about the guilt he harbored for putting the wheels of her situation into motion. This was about the fact that he liked her.

Primori or not, she was special.

"That's not right and you know it," he said fiercely. "There's a serial killer after her. She's not Primori, so rules shouldn't apply to her."

"I don't know what to tell you." Azagoth propped his hip on his desk and stretched his long legs out in front of him. "The Memitim Council only allows me to keep Sheoul-gra open to Memitim as long as they don't use it to thwart the Council's rules or to interfere with Primori fates."

"I'm not using Sheoul-gra for either of those things," he argued. "I have confirmation that Drayger's fate hasn't been changed by anything I've done with Aurora. Besides, this is your realm. Your rules. You can get the Memitim Council to change their minds. Make them."

"I can't, son," Azagoth said, and Hawkyn nearly fell over. Azagoth had never directly addressed him that way, and Hawkyn wasn't sure what to say. Fortunately, Azagoth continued speaking, sparing him a response. "There are only so many things I can negotiate for. I only have so many cards to play, and I can't waste them on a single human female."

"But—"

"No. You have a duty. A duty to your Primori. Not to a random human."

"She's neither random nor human," he gritted out. "And I don't need to be lectured about duty."

Azagoth's curse accompanied a sudden shove to his feet and a tangible tension in the air.

"You have feelings for this female. That's stupid, Hawk. You're letting your emotions affect the job. And your actions. It's a mistake."

"A *mistake*?" Hawkyn snorted. "I can't believe you just said that. You, who changed your entire realm for a female who seems to be avoiding you more often than not."

"My relationship with my mate is none of your concern."

A niggle of warning told Hawkyn he should shut up. Right now. But dammit, he liked Lilliana, his father had been a ginormous asshat recently, and his temper was already on the verge of eruption.

Azagoth's blood *did* flow in his veins, after all.

"It's a concern of mine when Lilliana's been more of a parent to me than you've ever been," he said. "I don't want to see her hurt."

Hissing, Azagoth rounded on him, and Hawk wondered what had pissed him off more; that Lilliana had been a better parent or that Hawkyn was accusing Azagoth of hurting her.

"I've provided you food, shelter, training—"

"Congratulations on doing the bare minimum, *Dad*. You going to take a bow for the six seconds it took you to ensure conception?" If the crimson rage in Azagoth's cheeks was any indication, this was a sore subject too, but Hawk was too worked up to hit the brakes. "At least my mother carried me inside her body before she dumped me in the human realm to fend for myself."

Azagoth went as still as an ice sculpture. "If you're so unhappy with your circumstances, why are you here?"

Good question. Until just a couple of years ago he'd resided with other Memitim in a Belgian castle, one of several "group homes" where Memitim lived and trained if they didn't want to live by themselves or serve Azagoth—pre-Lilliana, when he was still evil off-the-charts. But post-Lilliana, when their father opened up his realm to them, many, if not most, had come looking for something that had eluded the majority of them since birth—belonging to a family. A real parent. Brothers and sisters. And even though Azagoth could be a huge asshole, life in Sheoul-gra was still better than anything else Hawk had experienced.

"I'm not unhappy," he said. "Not here."

"But you *are* unhappy."

Hawkyn had never really thought about it like that. He'd been fucking great at his job, duty-bound to the point of ignoring even simple pleasures. But yeah, now that Azagoth mentioned it, he'd been increasingly dissatisfied with a lot of shit.

"I despise the bullshit Memitim rules. No alcohol besides wine. No sex. No self-gratification. Limited interaction with humans, demons, or angels who aren't Memitim. The fact that we're considered lesser angels, second-class citizens. I want to Ascend so I can become a Council member and change things. Did you know that some of the Council members are angels? Regular angels who were never Memitim? What kind of shit is that? How can they make the rules for people they don't respect or understand?"

Azagoth gave him a "duh" look because of course he knew angels sat on the Memitim Council. Hawk's mother was one of them.

"I understand your frustration," Azagoth said as he moved to the fully stocked bar, probably to rub Hawkyn's nose in the fact that he wasn't supposed to drink the fine rum he was reaching for. "Heaven has been making the rules for Sheoul-gra for thousands of years."

"And you bend and break them all the time."

"I know which ones can be altered." The rum made a soft gurgling sound as Azagoth poured it into a highball glass. "I know which are worth paying the price for."

"And you don't think allowing Aurora to stay here is worth the price."

"Nope." He took a swig of his drink. "Take my advice, son. Life is way too long to spend it with regrets. Send the female away and don't look back."

"Like you did with us? With our mothers?" It was a cheap shot, a throwaway line borne of hundreds of years of frustration. And maybe some abandonment issues.

"You know nothing," Azagoth growled. "I don't owe you an explanation."

"Actually, I think you owe me and my siblings a lot."

Azagoth's eyes began to glow with an unholy blood-red light, and Hawkyn knew he'd poked the beast one too many times. "Get. Out."

"Out of your office?" he snapped. "Or out of Sheoul-gra?"

"Your choice." There was no hesitation. No wavering of resolve in Azagoth's gaze or his voice. "But either way, get out of my sight, and take the female with you."

Hurt sliced through him. His father didn't give a flying fuck if he left. Well, maybe Hawk should take his advice. The one useful thing Azagoth had given him.

"No regrets, right?" He wheeled around and impulsively snatched the bottle of rum off Azagoth's bar top before opening the office door. "Don't look back."

He didn't.

But damn, it hurt.

Chapter Thirteen

Aurora had to get the hell out of here. There was no way she was going to sit around and wait for Hawkyn to serve her up to Drayger like a main course. If Drayger could, indeed, track her, she'd just keep moving until she could set up a trap to either kill him or bleed him.

Killing him would probably be impossible thanks to Hawkyn's protection, but if she could just get some blood, she could try Wytches_Float's instructions for breaking his ability to track. Of course, she'd need a sex partner for that too.

She suddenly pictured herself in bed with Hawkyn, his muscular body moving with hers, his strong hands touching her, stroking her, giving her the kind of pleasure she hadn't experienced in far too long. Feminine instinct told her he was the kind of male who would be dangerous in the sack, not because he was violent, but because he was addictive. She'd barely gotten a taste of him and she already understood that it would only take a single orgasm to get hopelessly hooked.

Snarling with frustration that was only partly sexual, she slipped out of Hotel Hell's side door. After checking to make sure no one was paying any attention, she secured her duffel on her shoulder and hurried toward the pad she and Hawkyn had arrived on. She didn't know how to operate it, but he'd said non-angels arrived and departed via a twin portal, so she had to try. How difficult could it be?

No one stopped her. Heck, no one even looked at her as she stepped onto the portal and planted her feet at the very center.

Nothing happened.

Was there a command? Or did it operate the way most of her abilities worked, with a mere thought?

Think.

She pictured a twin portal, and instantly, a rush of tingles spread through her insides. A tugging sensation came next, and the next thing she knew, she was looking at a forest, and this was definitely not Sheoul-gra.

But now what? There was a Harrowgate nearby, she was sure, but she wasn't sensitive to them and had no idea how to find it, let alone operate it.

She should have paid more attention when Runa escorted her through the one at Underworld General.

Well, she thought, as she considered her next move, at least she wasn't in Hell anymore. But if this was Siberia or some shit, it wouldn't be much better. She had no money, no identification, and no idea in which direction she should start walking.

Just as she was contemplating going back to Sheoul-gra, a tall male, his face concealed inside a hooded brown robe, popped onto the pad with her.

"Coming or going?" he asked.

"Ah...I guess it depends on your point of view." She eyed his robes and wondered if he was an angel, and if so, what kind. Weird, just days ago she hadn't been sure angels existed, and now she was aware that there were different varieties of them. "I'm trying to get to Portland, Oregon."

He stared at her with eyes so intense that she scrambled backward until her heels hit the edge of the pad. Power radiated from him in waves that crashed into her like an angry ocean and left it hard for her to breathe.

Was he going to hurt her? Her mind screamed for Hawkyn, and she didn't even care that she was in this situation because she had been trying to get away from him.

"Trust your instincts."

"What does that—"

A shower of light filled her vision, and a heartbeat later, she found herself standing in front of her house, her palms sweating, her heart pounding.

Jesus. How had she gone from living a relatively normal human life to bouncing around a supernatural landscape at the whim of beings she hadn't even believed in mere days ago?

She inhaled a ragged breath and tried to gather her thoughts. At least she was home. She could work with that.

It was night, but the full moon was so bright that it cast shadows all around her. Inside her house, the lights on a timer had come on, the faint glow streaming through gaps in the curtains.

On the surface, everything seemed normal. But as she moved toward the path to her front porch, a chill ran down her spine, nearly paralyzing her right there on her lawn.

Drayger.

Holy shit, he was inside her house. Inside her sanctuary.

Rage, terror, and the desire to take ugly, nasty revenge bubbled up in her throat where a war cry was on deck, ready to join the blast of silver fire she was going to send streaming into Drayger's chest. Her well of energy wasn't completely restored, but what she'd gotten from Hawkyn would be enough for one short burst. She just had to catch Drayger by surprise.

He knows you're here.

Yes, he probably did. But if she could hide, maybe sneak in—

The front door opened. Her fingertips burned as her power gathered. The second she saw his ugly face, he was toast.

"Aurora, no!"

Strong arms closed around her, and suddenly Hawkyn was there, his body between her and Drayger. Then, in a gust of cold wind, everything changed. The temperature. The time of day. The freaking *continent.*

She was no longer standing on her lawn, but on a cobblestone path. And she was no longer looking at her house, but a well-kept medieval castle.

"What the hell are you doing?" She tried to jerk away from Hawkyn's grip. "I was going to—"

"Kill him." Hawkyn released her and stepped back, his expression hard, cold, and despite her anger, she shivered. "You were going to kill him."

"Damn straight I was!" She cursed, releasing the hold on her power. As it drained from her fingers, her fury drained with it. Well, some of it, anyway. "Look, you have to protect him. I get that. But I need to live."

"What do you think I've been trying to make happen? That's why

I took you to the Gra."

"You're trying to keep me alive because you screwed up in the parking lot and you're trying to save your own skin. Can you blame me for trying to save mine? I'm not a pizza for you to deliver."

"Pizza?" He blinked. "What brought this on?"

"Does it matter? It's true, isn't it? If Drayger's fate requires me to die, you'll hand me over like a thin-crust pepperoni and you know it."

"Ham."

"What?"

"I like ham on my pizza. Not pepperoni."

She huffed. "The pizza isn't for you. That's the point."

"Your point is stupid," he said, sounding a little tired. "Listen to me, Aurora." He gripped her shoulders and dipped his head so his face was mere inches from hers, his gaze holding her in place even more so than his hands. "In the past, things might have been different. I've always done my job even if it didn't make sense. Even if I felt that what I was doing was wrong. But I'm invested in your well-being now. I'm invested in *you*. I *will* find a way to keep you safe. You're not a pizza. That's why we're here."

She eyed the castle, wondering if anyone was covertly watching them from the battlements or the arrow slits. "Why didn't you take me back to Sheoul-gra?"

He snarled. Actually *snarled*. "Because my father kicked us out."

"Oh." She certainly wasn't going to touch that topic right now. Seemed to be a little sensitive. But then, she'd be prickly too if her father had kicked her out of their home. She couldn't even imagine it, not when her parents were so loving and supportive. "So where, exactly, are we?"

He took her hand and started along the drawbridge that appeared to still be in working order. The moat beneath it teemed with... What the hell were those sharp-toothed, three-eyed things?

"We're in Belgium." His voice was still harsh with smoldering anger, but with every step they took, the tension eased in his body, his gait becoming looser, his shoulders pulling back. Her fingers itched to dig deep into those big muscles and massage the remaining stress away. "I lived here for a few hundred years, give or take a century."

A splash below drew her attention, and she looked down just as one of the dolphin-sized things in the water snapped its jaws, its three eyes focused on her like she was dinner. "Don't humans ask about the monsters in the moat?"

He laughed, a deep, lovely sound she appreciated even more after the earlier tension. "Those are horror-maws, sort of demon sharks that we use to keep enemies out when the drawbridge is up. And no, humans don't ask about them because this castle is hidden by an invisibility enchantment. No one can see it from outside the veil except Memitim. The only reason you can see it is that we're inside."

Even as he spoke, she swore she could feel the magic on her skin. A guard wearing a combination of modern military BDUs and plate armor waved them through the gate and into a massive courtyard where a dozen or so men and women sparred with various weapons.

"Everyone here is Memitim," he explained as they passed through a stone archway to the main building. "There used to be more of us here, but almost everyone has moved to Sheoul-gra. My brothers and sisters who remained are the few holdouts."

"Why would they be holding out?"

He shrugged, making his black T-shirt ride up so she got a glimpse of tan skin just above his waistband. "A lot of reasons, I guess. Sheoul-gra can be a bit claustrophobic and creepy. Plus, Azagoth can be an asshole." More anger billowed from him, but he seemed to put it back in some sort of container before he continued. "Some of my siblings have no desire to meet him. Ever. Can't say as I blame them."

Aurora couldn't help but be sad for him – for all of his siblings, and once again she counted her blessings that she'd grown up in a stable, happy family.

They approached a door with a brass plate that said "Admin," and he stopped. "I'll just be a minute. Don't run away again." He paused. "How did you get to your house, anyway?"

"I don't know. One moment I was standing on a landing pad thingie in a forest with a guy in hooded robes, and then I was home."

He frowned and then nodded. "Jim Bob. He arrived in Sheoul-gra just before my *heraldi* alerted me about Drayger being in danger." He shoved open the door. "I'll be right out."

He disappeared inside the office without explaining Jim Bob, so she wandered around the giant hall, marveling at the tapestries and portraits that depicted angels battling demons. All but one. The largest one, taking up nearly an entire wall, was of a stunning dark-haired man with piercing green eyes that seemed to look right through her. Shadows seemed to swirl around the picture, as if the man inside was swallowing the light both in the painting and in the room.

She heard footsteps behind her, knew instinctively it was Hawkyn. Or maybe she knew it was him because her heart fluttered every time he was close.

Oh, God, I'm attracted to an angel. An angel who is protecting the person who wants to slaughter me.

Really, that was pretty fucked up on more than one level.

"That's my father," he said, and she shivered. "Azagoth."

"I expected him to be hideous. This throws me off a bit." She glanced around at all the impossibly good-looking people walking around, including Hawkyn. "Does explain a lot, though. Your people are...beautiful."

"I'm guessing yours are, too?"

She felt her cheeks catch on fire. "Are you basing that on the fact that sex demons were used in our breeding, and sex demons are always attractive?"

"No," he said softly. "I'm basing that on you."

She sucked in a ragged, startled breath, but she didn't have time to respond, because a heartbeat later he was grabbing her bag and her hand and heading up a winding staircase.

"The housing administrator is giving you one of the two guest rooms on the top floor. They're nothing special, only a little larger than the Memitim rooms, but the bed is a double instead of a single and you have a private bathroom."

"Hawkyn!" A voice halted them in their tracks before they'd made it even halfway up the stairs.

"Fuck." Hawkyn released her hand and they both turned around.

Down below, in the great hall, stood two angels, their wings—one set black and the other light gray—extended as if getting ready to launch into the air. Both were holding scythes, and neither looked happy to be there.

Aurora gripped the handrail so hard her palm hurt. "Who are they?"

"They're Ascended brothers," he said calmly, but his tone didn't relieve the icy fear that filled her chest cavity. "And they're here to punish me."

* * * *

Hundreds of years ago, Hawkyn had waited, terrified and cornered, as men came to arrest him for stealing bread he'd needed to survive. He could still remember how hard his heart had pounded inside his thin body, how adrenaline had made his empty belly want to spill all over their shoes.

Shoes he didn't have.

He'd begged for mercy, but there had been none.

Now there were two Punishers from the Memitim embassy waiting for him below, but he was a different male. He would not cower. And he would not beg.

But this was not going to be fun.

"Stay here," he told Aurora as he dropped her bag on the steps. "No matter what happens, don't move." He took the steps down, keeping his eyes on the two males as he went. He'd never met these siblings, and even with the threat of violence hanging over his head, he still wondered which of the seventy-two angels Azagoth had bred with were their mothers. "Hello, boys. What brings you here?"

As if he couldn't guess.

Someone had ratted him out. Some asshole had reported that he'd interfered in his Primori's life, and he was going to get a thorough tongue lashing. Or maybe even a physical one.

"If you don't know, you deserve worse than what's going to happen to you." The taller of the two, the one with dark hair who was the spitting image of Azagoth, stepped forward. "I'm Leonas." He gestured to the ashen-haired male with the pale gray wings. "This is Moze."

"Nice to meet you," Hawkyn said, hoping they picked up every sarcastic note in his voice.

Moze snorted, but sobered at Leonas' glare.

"We are all full brothers, sons of Azagoth and Ulnara," Leonas said. "Which is probably why we were chosen to punish you for interfering with the actions of your Primori. Our superiors assumed you'd think we'd show mercy." Leonas smiled, the same icy smile their father used just before he turned someone into a living work of tortured art. "We won't."

Shit. This was going to be *way* worse than a tongue lashing or some sort of sanction.

Hawkyn summoned a weapon and threw up a personal shield, but even as his scythe formed in his palm, he knew that defense was futile. Ascended angels were far more powerful than any earthbound Memitim, and sure enough, he only got two swings of the blade in before Moze had him pinned against the wall, his face eating stone.

Roaring in anger, he kicked out, catching Moze in the upper thigh with a blow that would have broken a lesser male's leg. Moze shouted in pain, and then Hawk was the one in agony as Leonas smashed his fist into his back, right through his ribs. His fingers were like claws as they dug around until they found one of his shadow wings.

No!

Through his panting breaths and the spastic pounding of his pulse in his ears he heard Aurora's screams for his brothers to stop, but they didn't. Blood splashed to the floor as Leonas ripped the wing from its anchor and tossed it into the puddle at Hawk's feet. Like the shadow it was, it dissipated, leaving no trace at all.

Emerico, he thought, trying to focus on something besides the searing, tearing misery of Leonas' hand plunging inside him again to fish around for the remaining wing. Emerico was the one who had betrayed him. He wasn't sure how he knew that, but it made sense, and honestly, Hawkyn didn't blame him. Memitim were taught early in their training to put the rules and their duties ahead of everything else, including family and personal relationships.

For centuries Hawkyn had obeyed, being a good Memitim no matter what. He'd always wanted to do the right thing so he could join the Council and enforce the Memitim agenda.

Now he just wanted to burn the place down.

As Leonas tore Hawkyn's wing away, a lightning storm of pain wracked him, robbing him of his breath, his eyesight, and, mercifully, his consciousness.

Chapter Fourteen

"Lilliana!" Maddox's deep voice rang out from behind her as she sat on a quilt next to a pond that used to be black with bubbling tar. Now it was crystal clear and full of fish, and it was her favorite place to come with a romance novel and an iced tea once or twice a week. "*Lilliana!*"

She liked Maddox, even if he was a cocky jerk sometimes, and while he was excitable, he wasn't one to panic, so the alarm in his voice raised the hair on the back of her neck. Putting down her book, she twisted around to see him and Rico jogging toward her. Rico hung back a little, which was wise. It had been three months since he'd called her "Azagoth's whore," and she was still a bit raw.

But then, his face, where she'd slapped him, probably was too.

"What is it?"

Maddox skidded to a halt. "It's Azagoth. There was a Memitim Council member in his office with him. He just left and Azagoth is...not happy."

"Dammit," she breathed. "Okay, thanks. Where is he? Still in his office?"

"Library."

Her gut twisted. He loved the library. It was his place of comfort and one of two places—including the bedroom—where they had agreed there would be no anger. So why would he go there if he was upset? Something was wrong. Very, very wrong.

"Thank you." She came to her feet and flashed herself into the hallway outside the library.

Fully materialized, she coughed at the smoke filling the halls, streaming in tendrils from the scorched floors and walls. She didn't need to follow the blackened trail of Azagoth's fury to know it led from his office. He'd stormed from there to here, and she wasn't sure she wanted to see what was on the other side of the door.

Just knock. If he doesn't answer, hey, I tried.

She hated that she was willing to opt for avoidance rather than confrontation, but damn, his moods lately had been unlike anything she'd ever seen. Always before, she could ease him down off any ledge, but now it seemed like she only made things worse. She didn't know what to do, or who to talk to. Cat was a wonderful listener, but the fallen angel didn't have a lot of experience with relationships, and she and Hades had never even had a serious fight.

No, Lilliana was very alone in this.

Inhaling deeply, she rapped softly on the door.

No response.

Whew.

Feeling both guilty and relieved, she turned away, but froze when Azagoth's voice rumbled through the thick door.

"What?"

"Nothing," she called out. "I'll come back later."

He didn't say anything. What the hell? She should walk away, happy to escape, but dammit, his silence stung. Annoyed, she opened the door and stepped inside.

"Azagoth?" He was hovered over the miniature viewing stone she'd given him to keep an eye on his adult Memitim children who didn't live in Sheoul-gra. "Is everything okay? What's going on?"

He made a sound, something she imagined an angry bull might make. "They aren't going to give me my children." His big body shuddered, and her heart broke for him.

"Oh, darling, I'm so sorry." She reached for him, but he spun around to her, flames filling his eye sockets with so much heat she leaped backwards.

"This," he rumbled, "is your fault."

Stunned and confused by the accusation, she took another step back. "What are you talking about?"

"You made me soft." He grabbed his chest, right over his heart, his fingers digging in so fiercely his knuckles were white. "You made me feel."

She blinked. "Are you serious? The Memitim Council rejects your request and you're mad at *me*?"

"I wouldn't care about any of this if it weren't for you," he growled.

Her hurt veered sharply to annoyance at being blamed for such...stupidity. "Oh, well, gee," she snapped. "I'm so sorry I made you into a better person."

He swept his arm across his desk, knocking papers, pens, and books everywhere. He'd done that before, but he'd done it so they could have sex on the desk. Somehow she doubted they were going to be getting naked anytime soon.

"I'm not a better person!" His lips peeled back to reveal fangs he'd used on her to make her scream in pleasure but which now sliced down like weapons. "I'm distracted and angry. I can't stop thinking about how my children grew up. I hate it. I hate what I've become."

"I hate what you've become too," she said, practically choking on her words. They both hated what he'd become, but for different reasons. "But we can fix it."

He laughed, an ugly, cruel sound that made her cringe. "I've tried. Don't you think I've tried? Want to know how many hours I've logged in the Inner Sanctum? Want to know how much malevolence I've exposed myself to, the things I've done? Fuck, even Hades is useless."

Her mouth went so dry her tongue stuck to the roof of her mouth. She'd known he was angry, but she hadn't known he was angry at *her*, or that he was unhappy. Or that he'd been jonesing for some good old fashioned depravity.

"So that's it? You'd rather go back to how you were before I met you? Cold and emotionless? Evil?"

"It was easier!" he shouted.

"I see." She licked her lips, but it was like licking sandpaper with pumice. "Well, I hate to tell you this, but love is hard. Relationships are work. Anything that's worthwhile is."

"Yeah?" His rumbling laughter filled the room and sent chills across her skin. "That's all you've got? A lecture?"

So stubborn. "I've got love, Azagoth."

He snorted dismissively, and it was like a blow to the heart. "That's what got me into this mess."

Her sucker-punched heart squeezed painfully, and tears stung her eyes. They'd been through so much, and she'd been so patient with him. She knew his life wasn't an easy one and that he constantly struggled with the evil that surrounded him, and she could allow him a lot of leeway.

But she didn't deserve this.

"Fuck you," she rasped as she spun toward the door.

She wanted to rail at him, to hurt him the way he'd hurt her, but she didn't have the words or the breath. Anything more complex than telling him to get intimate with himself would make her break down into a sobbing mess.

She stumbled over her own feet as she flung herself out of the library, her watery, blurry eyes not helping anything at all.

"Wait! Lilliana, wait." Azagoth caught her by the arm and spun her around. "I'm sorry."

She jerked out of his grip. "I don't care. You don't get to say you regret loving me and then wipe it all away with two words."

"I didn't say I regret loving you."

"Semantics. Don't play that bullshit."

"I spent thousands of years being unable to feel, being unable to connect to anyone, and now I have all these children I want to know, but..." He jammed his hand through his hair so viciously she expected him to come away with tufts between his fingers. "Sometimes emotions overwhelm me and I don't know how to handle them. Yes, for a few moments I wanted to get rid of the pain. I just wanted to breathe for a second. But I've never once wanted to get rid of you. Please," he begged, falling to his knees in front of her. "I don't know how to do this."

Now she was the one growing soft. Seeing her big, powerful mate brought to his knees by grief tore her apart.

"You do what you did with me," she said gently. "You let your children in."

"But the guilt—"

She went to her knees in front of him, tears rolling down her cheeks now. "What's done is done. But look at the progress you've made. Look at what you're doing for your children now."

He snorted. "Yeah. Look what I'm doing to them. I sent Hawkyn away. I treated Idess and Mace like strangers. I want my young ones here and it pisses me off that the Council won't allow it, and yet, I'm a little relieved." His bloodshot eyes searched her face. "Why?"

Reaching up, she cupped his cheek. "Because you're afraid of losing control."

The flames licked at his pupils again. "I'm not afraid of anything."

"Nothing?" She stroked his jaw with her thumb, soothing, long strokes meant to bring him down, to give him a chance to think instead of react. "You're not afraid of losing all you've built here for yourself? Your children? Me? I think maybe your problem is the exact opposite. You have so much to lose that you can't help but be afraid of losing it. I know I would be." Leaning forward, she brushed her lips over his. "The key is to put aside the fear and just...live. You have a fabulous life, Azagoth. *We* have a fabulous life. And it'll only get better as we add to it. We'll find a way to locate your children and bring them here."

"I don't deserve you," he rasped.

"No, you don't," she teased, "but you got me, so we'll just have to find a way to deal with it."

Right there in the hallway, he tugged her against him, tucking her head against his shoulder as he held her. "I love you, Lilli. I love you so much."

"I love you too," she whispered. But sometimes she wondered if it was enough.

Something told her this wasn't over, and she didn't know if she was capable of giving him what he needed.

Chapter Fifteen

Aurora had never wanted to kill anyone as badly as she'd wanted to kill the bastards who had tortured Hawkyn and stripped him of his wings right in front of her eyes.

She'd actually tried. But even as she'd formed a ball of fire at her fingertips, the one called Moze had snuffed it. All he'd done was shift his gaze in her direction and her entire body went as stiff as a statue, completely immobilized. She'd been forced to watch in horror as the bastards ripped Hawkyn's amazing wings from his shoulders and tossed them to the bloody floor, where they'd withered and vanished.

Funny how she'd been as frozen as an ice sculpture but tears had still streamed down her cheeks in hot rivulets. How had Hawkyn endured the agony? Not just the physical pain, but the emotional misery of having his own brothers dismember him like that? She took back every negative thing she'd said or thought about her own brother, because truly, when it mattered, he'd been there for her. And she knew, without a doubt, that if she called him, he'd come to her, no matter what.

Hawkyn's family was the definition of dysfunctional, and her heart bled for him.

"Aurora?"

Hawkyn's scratchy voice jolted her out of her thoughts, and she put down the book a female named Jordan had given her to pass the time. Sure, she wouldn't have chosen a demon compendium as a beach read, but it had definitely occupied her mind. Who knew that raptor horrors enjoyed dining on pomegranates as well as people?

She hurried over to the bed Jordan and two other Memitim had laid Hawkyn's unconscious body on before cutting off his shredded, bloody shirt and tending to his wounds.

"How long..." he rasped as he pushed himself up on one elbow. "How long have I been out?"

"Half a day," she said, taking a seat on the stool next to the head of the bed. "I got some sleep over there." She gestured to the cot a Memitim whose name she didn't know had set up for her along the far wall. "I also got a shower and pancakes. Are you hungry? I can go down to the kitchen. It's two in the morning, but they said I can get anything I want."

For some reason, he smiled, amusement settling over features that had, just hours ago, been drawn in pain, even as he'd slept. "You're settling in, huh?"

"They've made it easy. I think they're rattled by..." She didn't want to say it. "By what happened to you. They're bending over backwards to be nice."

Jordan and another Memitim, a male called Drue, had seemed to think she needed company, and had shared a lot of Memitim and Heavenly history. She'd listened, fascinated, and if she hadn't been in dire need of sleep, she'd have loved to talk to them all night.

She reached for the pitcher of water on the bedside table. "Are you thirsty?"

"Yeah." He sat up with a wince and shoved the pitcher aside in favor of the bottle of vodka Jordan had left for him, along with a change of clothes.

He was going to look amazing in those black leather pants.

"Jordan said you guys aren't supposed to have any alcohol except wine, but that those Heavenly bastards waived the rule for you this once."

"How thoughtful." Anger practically bled from his pores as he unscrewed the cap and took a swig.

"I'm sorry," she said softly. "I couldn't help you. I tried, but..."

Swinging his legs over the side of the mattress, he glanced at the bucket of red-tinted water and the bloodstained rag she'd used to clean him up as he lay bleeding on the mattress. She'd been shocked at how quickly the deep lacerations in his back had healed, and she was even more shocked at how he was moving around just twelve hours later, as if nothing had happened.

"I hate that you had to see that." He cursed and shoved to his feet, the muscles in his arms and bare chest flexing with every motion. "I hate that all of this is happening to you. Drayger, having to hide, my asshole brothers. I'm sorry."

Startled by his apology when he was the one who had lost his wings for helping her, she poured herself a glass of water with a shaking hand. This was a male who she'd been convinced would deliver her to a serial killer if his duty required it, and yet he was clearly trying to protect her.

He'd lost his *wings* because of her.

I've always done my job even if it didn't make sense. Even if I felt that what I was doing was wrong. But I'm invested in your well-being now. I'm invested in you. I will find a way to keep you safe.

Shirtless, his jeans streaked with dried blood, he still managed to move with smooth, lethal grace as he paced the small room and drank from the bottle every dozen steps or so. "I'm going to request a Primori reassignment. I'm getting rid of Drayger."

Whoa. "You can do that?"

"Theoretically. But it's up to the Memitim Council. If they go for it, I won't have to protect Drayger anymore. He'll be some other Memitim's problem, and I can concentrate on keeping you safe."

"I—I don't know what to say. Thank you isn't enough." She swallowed, her eyes watering with gratitude. He'd lost his wings because he'd tried to save her from Drayger, and now this? She could never repay him. Not in a million years. But there *was* something she could do for him. "I know it's not much, but I can take away your pain if you want."

"I'm not in pain." He guzzled a good fifth of the bottle.

"Yeah," she said, "you are. And I can take it away. Well, it won't be completely gone, but it'll be manageable."

"I'm fine." His voice pitched low with a dark, alcohol-soaked rasp. "I'm healed."

She moved to him, planting her palm on his sternum, careful to keep her energy siphon turned off. She didn't need the mind-scrambling incoherency right now.

"I'm not talking about physical pain, and I think you know that." Tentatively, she eased her hand to the right, covering his heart. It thudded faster now, his pulse pounding into her palm as if trying to match the cadence of her own heartbeat. "I can help. Please, let me help."

A battle warred in his expression, a look she'd seen before, back when her brother had come home from a mission that haunted him. He'd wanted to talk, but his pride, or maybe his military orders, hadn't let him.

"No one has ever helped me before," he said, his single-barrel-whiskey smooth voice turned rotgut-vodka rough. "No one but my siblings."

"You lost your wings because you helped me." She stepped back so she didn't have to crane her neck to look up at him and so he could see every genuine emotion on her face. "Jordan explained how much of a risk it was, and what you stand to lose by breaking rules. I don't understand this Memitim Council thing, but it sounds like there's nothing more you want than to sit on it and change things for the better. So let me do this for you. It's the one thing I'm really, really good at."

For a long, torturous moment, he said nothing. Then, finally, the hard set of his shoulders relaxed, although the wariness in his eyes remained.

"How?"

Man, she needed a drink for this, and his vodka looked tasty. "There's a reason I'm a masseuse," she said, holding out her empty water glass with a gesture at his liquor bottle. As he poured a generous couple of shots, she continued. "I recharge my powers through touch. I absorb negative energy and emotions and turn them into fuel for my abilities." She sipped her drink, enjoying the sting of alcohol on her lips. "My clients leave feeling happy and lighter, and I'm now Portland's most in-demand masseuse."

And not just Portland. Spas all over the country wanted to hire her, offering her more money, places to live, exclusive client lists. She'd even been approached by the owner of a world-renowned Swedish resort and a Hollywood celebrity wanting a personal live-in masseuse. Thanks, but no thanks. She liked her quiet life of obscurity and didn't want to move. Portland suited her. With its quirky and laid-back personality, world-famous restaurants and breweries, and endless things to do, the city felt like home the way Sacramento, where she'd grown up, never had.

"So you want to give me a massage?""

"That's one method. It's the slow one." She paused for a heartbeat and then, before she changed her mind, blurted, "There's also a fast one."

"Yeah?" He took a swig of vodka, the tendons in his throat undulating with each swallow. "What the hell. Let's do the fast one."

"Don't you even want to know what it is?"

"I don't care what it is. My father kicked me out of his realm, I probably lost any chance I had to sit on the Memitim Council, and two brothers I'd never met just dug my wings out of my body with their bare hands." He barked out a bitter laugh. "Fuck it. I can handle anything. Just do it."

Abruptly, her body flushed with heat, but her brain balked. She generally avoided the second method, the one that was the hallmark of her succubus heritage. It was too intense. Too intimate. When her partner orgasmed, more than just his seed rushed into her body. She got a blast of power so pleasurable that it would send her into an extended orgasm of insane pleasure, but she also got a head full of emotions that came with little or no context. There might be a mix of sadness, anger, love, jealousy... And unless her partner told her everything he was feeling ahead of time, she was left with a knot of emotions that tangled her up inside for hours. It was one of the reasons she'd avoided relationships.

But damn... Hawkyn tempted her. Yes, he was angry right now, but angels were good, right? How much emotional baggage could there possibly be?

No one has ever helped me before.

Okay, maybe there was a lot. Everyone she'd talked to had mentioned that Memitim grew up in the most atrocious situations imaginable, and even after they'd been plucked from the human world and introduced to the work they'd been bred to do, life still didn't seem that great. How could it be when you had no choice about how you lived or the job you were doing? She might have gone into the spa business because it seemed like a good way to collect the energy she needed to survive, but the truth was that she enjoyed it. She liked making people feel good. Happy, positive people were what the world needed. And from what she'd seen, Memitim could especially use some sort of underworld spa.

"Well?" He stared at her from across the room, his hand wrapped in a death grip around the bottle, his gaze holding the same smoldering intensity she'd seen in his father's eyes in the portrait downstairs.

God, what was it going to be like to have all that intensity focused on her? Touching her? Inside her? All he had to do was look at her and she shivered with violent tingles.

The cold air in this drafty castle just got warmer. "Okay, but don't say I didn't warn you."

"You didn't."

"Didn't what?"

"Warn me."

She huffed. "When I said not to say I didn't warn you... I was warning you."

His lazy, lopsided smile made her groan. He was teasing her. She loved these glimpses, brief as they were, into his off-duty personality. He'd been on the go since they'd met, in a constant state of motion, and despite the shitty circumstances, it was nice to see him relax a little.

Of course, that could have something to do with the ninety-proof bottle of attitude adjuster in his hand.

She eyed her own glass of liquid bravery, but really, she didn't need it. Even if her succubus genes weren't already going to work, preparing her body with a hot rush of desire, she'd want Hawkyn.

And she'd want to help him.

As he gulped down another swig of vodka, she set her glass on the little end table and turned to him.

"Here's another warning." She pulled her shirt up over her head. "Some scenes may be too intense for young viewers." She tossed the shirt onto the mattress and reached around to unhook her bra.

"What are you doing?" he croaked, the vodka bottle frozen a few inches from his mouth.

"Sex. That's the fast method." She dropped the bra on the mattress and flushed at the way he stared at her exposed breasts. "You game?"

For a long, tortured moment, he said nothing. Oh, God, what if he refused her? How embarrassing. She'd made a huge mistake, and she looked like a desperate fool. Choking on humiliation, she lifted her hands to cover herself, but he shook his head.

"Don't." His voice was a low growl, sultry and dark, so resonant it hit her between her legs. "You're beautiful."

"Does this mean—"

He was on her before she could finish. His lips came down on hers and his body pressed her into the cold stone wall and both his hands gripped her shoulders so firmly she figured she'd have bruises later.

Awesome.

Chapter Sixteen

Hawkyn was going to do this. He was going to fucking do this. Sex with his first female in centuries. He was going to break all the damned Memitim rules, and he was going to do it well.

And he was going to do it with the amazing female standing in front of him. A female who had every right to hate him for his role in protecting the violent murderer who was hunting her. Hell, he was starting to hate himself.

Her hands gripped his waist, and the self-loathing drained away, replaced by a searing need he hadn't felt in a long time. No, he'd never felt this, the driving desire to be with someone not as a temporary escape, but as an all-in experience. What happened between them might not be the first step to forever, but as a Memitim, he couldn't have that with anyone but another angel anyway.

The sudden idea that he would mate with an angel one day jolted him. He'd assumed he'd pass all his Memitim tests, do his job on Earth admirably, and join the Council before settling down with a female. But as Aurora's lips nibbled his jaw and her hands caressed the sensitive skin on his back where his wings had once been, all he could think about was being with her.

He didn't even care if she could ease his pain. It didn't matter. He'd spent his entire Memitim life taking care of others, others who didn't deserve it. Every scumbag he guarded ate a bit of his soul, and it was high time he did something life-affirming for himself.

See, this was the kind of thing he'd change if he made it onto the Memitim Council.

Except that he knew damned well that wasn't going to happen

anymore, and the feeling of loss in the space where his wings should be made that achingly clear.

"No," he gasped, breaking away from her. He stumbled backward, knocking over the TV tray in the corner and sending it crashing to the floor. His vodka bottle shattered, spraying alcohol everywhere.

"Hey," Aurora said, alarm flickering in the depths of her ocean-blue eyes. "What's wrong? Are you okay?"

No, he wasn't. He was a fucking head case. "Yeah," he breathed. "Yeah. Sorry. I'm just... It's been a long time."

"For me too," she said quietly.

"How long?"

"A few years. You?"

He snorted. "A few centuries." A few *long* centuries.

"Seriously?" She moved toward him, her full breasts bouncing tantalizingly with each step. "Wow."

"We have to take a vow of celibacy."

"Damn," she breathed, stopping in her tracks. "Then we can't do this."

"The hell we can't. I just have to get out of my own head."

"You're worried about the punishment, aren't you?"

He snorted again. "I don't give a shit about it. I'm sick of the damned rules. I'm sick of the bullshit."

"Then what is it?"

"You know what?" he asked as he closed the distance between them. "It's nothing. It's absolutely nothing."

Because fuck it. The moment he'd flashed into the dark parking lot and interfered in Aurora's abduction, he'd known on some level that he was tempting fate. He'd told himself he was cool with guarding evil people, but now he could admit to himself that over the years a hairline fracture had formed in the compartment where he'd kept his indifference.

And when he'd seen Aurora, that fracture had led to a complete shatter, just like that vodka bottle on the floor.

She moaned as he covered her mouth with his and walked her backward until she bumped against the wide stone window ledge. He hadn't done this in a long, long time, but sex didn't have a steep learning curve and he'd always been a self-starter.

Still kissing her, he cupped her breasts, circling her nipples with his thumbs. She gasped in response, arching into his touch and thrusting her pelvis against his aching erection.

"We're not naked enough," she whispered against his lips, and he agreed.

His breath came faster as he dropped one hand to her waistband and ripped her jeans open. Her fingers fumbled with his fly until the buttons popped and his cock, swollen and stiff, sprung into her waiting grip.

He nearly came right then and there. "Easy, there, little Wytch," he croaked. "My fuse has been on a slow burn for hundreds of years. Won't take much to set me off—"

Suddenly, she dropped to her knees, shoved his jeans down to his thighs and swallowed him. Just swallowed him whole. The tip of his cock hit the back of her throat and he yelled out in sheer, electric pleasure.

"What are you doing?" he rasped as she flicked her tongue back and forth over his shaft.

She sucked upward hard, and his erection came free of her hot mouth with a soft pop. "I'm taking the edge off. Besides, you need at least two orgasms for the full effect of my magic to work."

"Seriously?" Not that he was going to argue with that.

She graced him with a flirty, wicked smile that suited her. "No. I just want to know what an angel tastes like when he comes."

He'd have laughed if he wasn't on the verge of giving her what she wanted. As it was, he had to bite his tongue, concentrating on the pain rather than the pleasure of her fingers as they caressed his sac. She lowered her mouth to him again, her tongue flicking over the head of his cock.

Adrenaline surged through him, spiking his desire as his balls tightened and a tingle spread through his shaft. He was close, so close his legs were rubber and he had to throw out a hand to catch himself on the wall so he didn't collapse on top of Aurora.

He dared not look down at the erotic sight of her sucking him. Instead he closed his eyes and concentrated on the feel of her wet mouth sliding up and down. Of her tongue circling his mushroom head. Of her lips nibbling his balls while her fingers stroked the shockingly sensitive skin just behind them.

And when she increased the pressure, her fingers massaging,

kneading, squeezing, a vibration unlike anything he'd ever experienced shot through him like a strike of erotic lightning—and that was when she took him to Heaven.

Screw the rules. He didn't need to Ascend to get what he needed. Or what he wanted.

He drowned in bliss, pumping his hips as she pumped with her fist, and holy hell, Aurora was, for him, the pinnacle of Heaven.

* * * *

In Aurora's experience, when a guy came, he needed a minute to recover. More than a minute, actually.

So she was shocked as hell when, just moments after his powerful orgasm that overloaded her senses with the blast of energy, he withdrew from her mouth, hauled her to her feet, and tore her pants off like they were made of tissue paper.

His emotions filtered through her, his anger and pain converting to positive power much faster than had ever happened in the past. Usually the negativity lingered, sometimes for days, but like everything else about Hawkyn, his energy was unique. Addictive. She wanted more.

"That was incredible," he growled as he tossed aside the shredded jeans, leaving her only in aqua panties with lovely black lace—that Hawkyn bit through with his fangs.

She shivered, despite the fiery need flowing through her veins, consuming her as it built into an inferno she was sure would scorch them both.

His big hands palmed her thighs, spread them as he eased her back onto the windowsill. His emerald eyes glowed with erotic light as he took her in. Was he going to... *Yessss.*

His tongue speared her center, stabbing deep before he dragged it up, licking her swollen, sensitive tissues. She cried out, his name carrying through the small space, and she felt him smile against her core.

"I don't have any experience with this," he said in a raw, ragged voice, his hot breath tickling the skin of her inner thigh, "but I learn fast."

Which he proved by latching on to her clit and drawing on it gently, using her moans and panting breaths as a guide. A finger penetrated her, pumping and flicking, and she had to bite down on the heel of her palm to keep from screaming in ecstasy.

The orgasm hit her like a sudden tempest, tearing her world apart before it all came together again with Hawkyn climbing up her body and settling himself between her legs as she sat on the stone ledge.

When had he taken off his pants?

Not that she cared about details like that. Not when he was staring down at her with half-lidded, possessive eyes that burned with male need. God, when he looked at her like that, he could have anything he wanted.

Anything. Anything except... "Wait," she breathed. "Protection."

"Memitim aren't fertile." The tip of his shaft prodded her entrance, but he hesitated, waiting for permission. "Not until we Ascend."

"Okay, then." She leaned back against the thick, opaque glass in the window and spread her legs wider. "That's exactly what I wanted to hear."

"Damn," he breathed as he pushed inside her. "You're so beautiful. So perfect."

No, what was perfect was the way he was so careful with her. His erection slid inside her slowly, stretching her exquisitely as he watched her, his gaze roaming her expression for every reaction.

When he was fully seated, he framed her face in his hands, holding her for his kiss. She took it eagerly, slipping her tongue between his lips as he started to move against her. In seconds, the kiss flared hot and urgent, and a rumble of approval rattled deep in his chest.

His tongue slid against hers, stroking and thrusting, the tempo matching the rocking of his hips. Tension mounted between her legs as she locked her thighs around his waist, holding him where she needed him to be.

This was perfect. So perfect. Like everything about him. She slid her palms up from his waist to his perfectly healed back, charting the hills and valleys of his muscles, the heavy bone structure, the ropey tendons. This was her playground, and as he took her higher with every thrust, she used her fingers to knead all the pleasure points within her reach, loving how he gasped when she dug deep.

As a masseuse, she knew the benefits of massage. But as a Wytch, with sex demon ancestors, she also had unique knowledge that allowed her to access erogenous zones most people didn't even know they had.

She used that knowledge now with precision and skill, loving how, when she knuckled a spot between his third and fourth rib, he moaned. Or when she used two fingers on a pressure point in the ridge of his shoulder, his entire body spasmed, his head falling back in a vision of male ecstasy.

"You're killing me," he whispered. "Fuck, you're amazing."

Abruptly, he swept her up and, still sheathed inside her, he carried her over to the bed. His strength as he lowered her left her in awe.

Panting with desperate need, she pulled him down so they were chest to chest, her legs wrapped around his waist in a hold she wouldn't let him break anytime soon.

She'd had sex before, obviously, and her succubus nature had been all about the pleasure for a purpose. Sex and magic were a release. But what she was doing with Hawkyn had gone beyond that. It might have started as a way to help him get rid of the negativity and pain that weighed him down, but now it was about being with him. About giving him a piece of herself.

She'd never done *that* before.

He rocked against her, plunging deep before driving a series of rapid, short strokes into her clenched core. His thick shaft rubbed her in just the right places as she arched into him, taking him as fast, as hard, as deep as he could go.

Her fingernails scored his back as he rotated his hips, and she couldn't stop looking at his face, at the sweat glistening on his brow, at his jaw clenched in the most male of ecstasies, at his lips that had given her so much pleasure parted for his labored breaths.

At this moment, he seemed to be both angel and demon, because what he was doing to her was nothing short of evil, but he was so damned good at it.

"Now," she whispered as she bucked against him. "Please..."

As if he'd been waiting for permission, he lunged, his pelvis slamming into her so hard she slid up the mattress and bumped her head against the headboard. The thing began to bang on the wall, but if it bothered him, it didn't show.

He pounded into her, showing no mercy, but she didn't want it. She wanted all of him. All of that lovely power and all of that immense strength.

"Yes," she cried. "Right...*there.*"

He jerked, his body going taut as he roared in release. Hot splashes of semen warmed her from the inside and triggered her own climax. Her body seized, wracked by waves of pleasure so intense she thought she might pass out. She struggled to focus, to stay conscious so she didn't lose a single second of the ecstasy that was utterly shattering. Life-altering.

Good...God.

Hawkyn's heavy weight came down on her, and she welcomed it. It might be the only thing keeping her from floating away on a cloud of bliss.

Again, the emotional transfer of negativity sifted through her, individual threads of anger and sadness that made sense, given the fight with his father, the torture at the hands of his brothers, and the conflict he felt over choosing her safety over his duty to his Primori. She inhaled, counting through a breathing exercise that helped convert negative emotions to positive energy, and within moments, peace surrounded her in a cocoon of warmth.

"This feels so right," he murmured roughly, one hand stroking her hair as he lay on top of her. "I should be regretting this right now. I should be laden with guilt and wondering what the Memitim Council is going to do to me, but I honestly just don't care."

"See? I absorbed all that negative energy and pain—" She broke off as what he'd just said sunk in, and alarm shot through her. "Wait. What they're going to do to you? What do you mean?"

Smiling, he shifted but tucked her against him so they were one big side-by-side tangle on the bed. "It's nothing you need to worry about. Whatever happens, it's mine to deal with."

That wasn't fair, but the mind-blowing sex and the events of the last few days had caught up with her, and all she wanted was a chance to rest in the strong arms of an angel. Just for a little while.

They could deal with all the other shit later.

And something told her there was going to be a lot of it.

Chapter Seventeen

Aurora woke up sore, but in that amazing way that made her want to stay in bed all day. Except that Hawkyn wasn't in bed with her.

Rubbing her eyes, she sat up. He hadn't left a note, but he'd clearly showered and dressed. Where was he? And how the hell had he done all of that without her waking up? She'd always been a heavy sleeper, but geez, she must have been exhausted.

Which made sense, given that she'd barely slept since Drayger had captured her. Closing her eyes meant seeing the things he did to her on the backs of her eyelids. Sleeping meant nightmares. But she hadn't had any last night.

Maybe sleeping in the arms of an angel kept the bad things away.

She could get used to that.

Yawning, she climbed out of bed and headed toward the bathroom, but after a couple of steps she swayed, a wave of nausea rocking her hard. Whoa. Maybe the vodka had been stronger than she'd thought. Another hot wave hit her, and she stumbled into the bathroom, her head spinning, her gut rolling. What was happening? Was it something she ate? Sketchy Memitim pancakes?

Bracing herself on the edge of the sink, she turned on the faucet and splashed icy water on her face. Much better.

"Aurora?" Hawkyn tapped on the door. "You okay?"

"I'm fine," she called out. She looked into the mirror and cringed at the crazy case of bedhead and the dark circles under her puffy eyes. "Fine" might have been an overstatement.

"Breakfast is ready. I can bring up a tray if you don't want to eat in the great hall."

"No," she said, reaching for a towel. "Go on down. I'll meet you in a few minutes."

"You sure?"

"I managed going down the stairs when you were passed out." She turned off the water. "I think I'll be okay."

His deep chuckle filtered through the door. "I'll have coffee waiting."

Her stomach rebelled, but she thanked him anyway. She spent the next ten minutes getting cleaned up, and by the time she was dressed in the navy leggings, belted cream tunic, and casual flats she'd packed, she was feeling a hundred percent again. Well, ninety-nine, at least. She still didn't think coffee sounded good.

She found Hawkyn in the great hall, seated at the end of one of the two trestle tables lining the walls. A few Memitim were gathered around him, full of questions—mostly about Azagoth and Sheoul-gra, if the number of times those names were thrown around was any indication.

Aurora's heart squeezed painfully. She couldn't help but feel sad for them, and she vowed to call her parents soon, if for no other reason than to tell them she loved them. She couldn't imagine not knowing her father, who had patiently taught her math and how to fish, or her mother, who had been liberal with hugs and jokes. But then, she couldn't imagine having the Grim Reaper as a parent. She had to give Hawkyn credit, though; as angry as he was with Azagoth, he didn't badmouth him to his siblings. If anything, he downplayed his own issues with his father and encouraged everyone to decide for themselves.

It made her admire him even more.

As she approached the group, she turned her attention to the trays of fruit and pastries that crowded the center of the table. Even better, the mouthwatering aroma of eggs, cheese, and ham wafted from two steaming warmers and a platter.

The sight of the coffee pitcher, however, turned her stomach. Wendy, the barista at Hot Beans down the street from Aurora's place, would be shocked. Aurora couldn't pass the place without a triple-shot caramel cappuccino.

Hawkyn turned to her, his lips curved into a secret smile. The things those lips had done... God, he could do them over and over.

"Aurora, hey, I saved you a—" He broke off, his mouth open, his face draining of blood.

"Holy shite!" A red-haired Memitim who couldn't be older than twenty gaped at her, his freckles standing out starkly against his ivory skin. "She's...she's..."

"What?" She looked down at herself, searching for evidence that she'd grown another limb or a horn or an all-over body rash, but she couldn't see anything unusual. But now *everyone* was staring. Staring like she'd, well, grown another limb, a horn, or a rash. "What am I?"

Then she saw it. Her fingernails. They were turning silver, as if she'd applied a coat of glittery nail polish. She gasped, a thread of panic wrapping around her like a noose. This was bad. And...impossible.

"Hawkyn." Drue, who had been so friendly and accommodating last night, turned his accusing gaze on her. "Man, you need to get her out of here. Now."

Confusion tamped down her immediate panic. "Why? What's going on?"

Hawkyn leaped up from the table, took her hand, and practically dragged her up the stairs. "We have to pack. We have to get you out of here."

"Hawkyn!" She jerked him to a halt at the threshold of the room they'd stayed in last night. "I'm not going anywhere until you tell me why we need to leave."

"Because Primori aren't allowed here," he said, troubled shadows flitting in his eyes. "And you're Primori."

"*What?*"

He stormed inside the room, his motions jerky and stiff as he packed her duffel. "This is crazy." Outside the window, a storm was brewing, and it felt as if one was brewing inside, too. "Between last night and this morning, something happened to make you Primori."

Recalling this morning's fit of illness, she looked down at her nails.

"I...think I might know what it was," she said, nausea welling up again, but this time she was sure it was coming from nerves.

He rounded on her, his body taut, his expression etched with concern. "Tell me."

Holding her belly with one hand to quell the butterflies, she held up the other, showing him her silver nails, a telltale sign among her people.

"I don't understand." He scowled at her hand. "Do you think painting your nails did it?"

"I didn't paint them. And there's no easy way to say this," she said in a voice that quaked like the tree outside the window being buffeted by the wind, "but..."

"But what?"

She hesitated. Shifted her weight. And then blurted words she hadn't thought she'd say for a long, long time.

"I'm pregnant."

* * * *

I'm pregnant.

Pregnant. Holy shit.

Hawkyn stumbled backward, banging the backs of his legs into the bed he and Aurora had made love in last night. But there was no way he could have impregnated her. Memitim weren't fertile. There had to be another explanation.

She was watching him with glassy eyes, and he realized she was just as stunned as he was. She'd gone through so much recently, and then to add this to the mix... Damn.

"You said you haven't had sex in a long time." At her nod, he continued, somehow managing to sound calm instead of freaked out. "Is it possible that your species has an extended gestation period? I've heard that some female demons hold sperm inside their bodies for years before it fertilizes an egg. And others—"

"No," she said sharply. "That's not what's going on. Wytches are, for the most part, just like humans." She looked down at her hands. "Except for the silver nails."

"You're sure." He swallowed, buying time to process this. It didn't help. "You're positive that I'm the father."

She glared. "I'm sure. This is your doing, Hawkyn."

His legs gave out, and he sank down on the mattress. He had truly never thought about having kids. Not when it could be hundreds, or even thousands, of years before he Ascended, became fertile, and took a mate. This wasn't just unexpected; it was unprecedented.

And he was in a shitload of trouble.

This would end in his expulsion from the Memitim order. He'd be stripped of his powers and left to live in the human realm for eternity.

The human realm. With Aurora. And his child.

Maybe...maybe it wouldn't be so bad.

"Look," she said as she finished packing her duffel. "I've learned enough about Memitim from you, Suzanne, Lilliana, and the people here to know that this is probably really, really bad for you. No one has to know that you're the father—"

He didn't even know he'd made the decision to flash himself to her until he found himself in front of her, his hands on her slender shoulders, his face in hers.

"That," he growled, "is not an option. I grew up without a father, and that will *never* happen to any child of mine. We'll get through this, Aurora. Things might be a little rough until we get it all figured out, but we'll do it."

Tears shimmered in her eyes, and dammit, he couldn't handle it if she cried. Gently, he lowered his mouth to hers and kissed her, tentatively at first, letting her decide if this was what she wanted. Did she want his kiss? Did she want *him*?

His pulse raced as he waited for more than her passive kiss. He wanted the passion she'd brought to bed last night. The passion she had for life and all that came with it.

Nothing. She stood stiffly, her spine as straight as a sword, her pulse fluttering in the vein in her temple.

Please, Aurora.

He increased the pressure on her mouth, using his tongue to stroke the seam of her lips, and finally, blessedly, she responded. With a moan, she sagged against him, wrapping her arms around him and opening up to his kiss.

This was what he'd wanted his entire life, even if he hadn't known it. He'd lived for duty, never for himself, and for the first time, he understood his sister Suzanne's desire for a life and interests outside of the confines of Sheoul-gra.

The problem was that it wasn't possible. Not for Memitim. Idess was proof of that. She'd lost her angel status and was all but human now.

Idess is happy.

Yes, she was. But Hawkyn knew himself well enough to know

that, while he could survive being expelled from the Memitim order, especially if he had Aurora and a family, he would always have regrets. He'd always wonder if he should have done things differently. Because he wanted it all. He wanted Aurora and the life she carried inside her. But he also wanted to serve on the Memitim Council.

He couldn't have both, and he knew it.

Reluctantly, he pulled back and gazed into Aurora's drowsy eyes. "We have to get you someplace where you're allowed as Primori."

"How about my home? Can we at least stop by there so I can check mail and pack a few more things? We left in such a rush last time." She rolled her bottom lip between her teeth. "If you think it'll be safe for a little while."

He started to object, but her new status had just changed things. She would never be safer than she was right now.

"You're Primori, so you have your own guardian angel." But who? He was going to need to find out. He hated to admit it, but some of his siblings were far more reliable than others, and he wanted Aurora to have only the best.

"No," she said, putting her palm on his chest. "I have two."

Yes, she did. For as long as he was still an angel, anyway. He had a feeling his time had become very, very short.

Chapter Eighteen

Hawkyn flashed them both to her house, but he kept her close as he cleared the place to make sure there were no signs that Drayger had set a trap or was hiding in a closet. Once Hawkyn gave the all-clear, she nearly collapsed in relief.

It was good to be home. She was exhausted, mentally tied up in knots, and she'd kill for a cup of chamomile tea.

"Are you hungry?" She headed for the kitchen, her stomach rumbling. She'd missed breakfast, thanks to the fact that she'd suddenly become pregnant and Primori, and the Memitim at the castle had kicked them out. Nicely, but still.

Jordan had even given her a hug.

"Hungry? No. I can't even think about eating right now. I don't like being out in the open like this."

"You said it yourself. I have a guardian angel, right? So if Drayger shows up, won't my new angel sense it?"

"Yes, but—" He flinched and looked down at his arm. For a long moment, he simply stared.

"Hawkyn?" His silence was starting to scare her. "What is it?"

"It's Drayger." His mouth curved slowly into a grim smile that gave her chills. "He's no longer Primori."

She sucked in a startled breath. "Seriously? What...what does that mean, exactly?"

"It means he's no longer under angelic protection. Mine or otherwise."

Afraid to hope but hoping to no longer be afraid, she studied every micro-expression on Hawkyn's face for signs that there was a catch to what he was saying. But his eyes glittered, his fangs gleamed, and he was smiling like he'd won the lottery.

"So he can pay for what he's done?"

He nodded. "We can alert the police." His gaze turned dark with bloodthirsty anticipation that sent a fresh wave of chills across the surface of her skin. "Or I can kill him."

Oh, yes. She wanted that. Holy shit, it frightened her how much she wanted that. But she wasn't Drayger's only victim. There were a lot of families out there who needed justice and closure.

As if Hawkyn sensed her inner turmoil, he folded her into his arms.

"I'll take care of it," he murmured against her hair. "I'll make him feel everything he did to you and the others."

"No," she said, pulling back so she could see him. "He needs to be caught. He needs to pay for what he's done, but it needs to happen through the human justice system."

"But—"

"No." She pressed her fingers to his lips, silencing him when part of her really wanted him to convince her that his way, the deadly way, would be better. "It's for the families of his other victims. They need closure. But he'll pay the true price after he's dead, won't he?"

"Oh, yes." A vengeful light glittered in his eyes. "He's evil, so he'll go straight to my father's realm. I'll make sure he pays for all eternity."

She shivered.

"I'm sorry," he said, regret turning his voice rough. "I scared you."

"Oh, no," she whispered. "You turned me on."

Hawkyn pegged her with an amused look. "In that case, before we call 911, let me tell you what I did to a demon who I once caught breaking into an orphanage..."

* * * *

Hawkyn was going to be there when the police arrived to arrest Drayger. They should be at his house at any moment, and Hawk couldn't wait. He just had to resist the urge to kill him before the cops got there. If Aurora gave him the go ahead, he'd slaughter that fucker in a heartbeat. Sure, killing a human was forbidden, but so was just about everything he'd done since the moment he'd flashed into the grocery store parking lot and found Drayger in the middle of an attempted abduction.

Hawkyn was so over following the rules. If Aurora changed her mind and wanted Drayger dead, the guy was going to die.

Unfortunately, she was adamant about letting the bastard live long enough to pay for his crimes in jail, so both he and Aurora set wards around her house, allowing him to leave for a few minutes without worrying. Between the wards and her new guardian—whoever it was—she was as safe as could be expected. He doubted he could have left her anyplace safer, actually.

He kissed her, promising to be back within minutes. Without his shadow wings, he had to manually engage the *shrowd* with a command, and then he flashed inside Drayger's living room. But before he'd fully materialized, the stench of blood and terror stung his nostrils.

Something was wrong. Horribly wrong.

Cursing, he summoned a weapon to the ready, an electrical shock that would stun anyone—or anything—he encountered.

Noises came from the back of the house...crying? He moved down the hall, slowing at the trickle of blood that flowed from the master bedroom.

Fuck. A sharp, piercing ache pounded in his chest. If Drayger had slaughtered another female, Hawkyn would never forgive himself. Steeling himself for the worst, he stepped inside the room.

Turned out that there was no way he could have prepared himself for the bloodbath in front of him. The walls, ceiling, furniture, everything was splattered—and it wasn't just blood. Bits of flesh, entrails, and even teeth had found their way into all of the nooks and crannies.

And all of it belonged to Drayger. The leg on the bed. The arm on the floor. The other arm hanging from the ceiling fan. Hawk didn't want to know where his head was.

Damn, this house was going to have to be torn down, because no one was going to want to live here after these crime scene photos got out.

A noise startled him, and he spun, instinctively summoning a scythe. A female, naked and covered in gore, huddled in the closet, one hand pressed against a nasty gash in her thigh. She looked familiar, but why?

He stepped out of the *shroud* and became fully visible. She didn't even look surprised. Her glazed eyes took him in with wariness but not fear.

"Who are you?" She scurried out of the closet, putting more space between them and moving closer to the door. "Are you going to kill me?"

"Kill you? What? No." He spoke softly, afraid to spook her. "I came here to make sure he didn't hurt anyone else. Are you all right? Did he hurt you?"

Flexing her fingers like a cat, she growled, a deep, throaty sound he wouldn't have been surprised to hear from a tiger. "Not this time, he didn't."

"So *you* did this?" When she didn't answer, he took a closer look at the carnage, and suddenly, her mannerisms made sense, especially when matched with the claw and teeth marks on the body parts and the ripped women's clothes on the floor. "You're a shifter. Lion or tiger. Right?" Shifters often destroyed their clothing when they morphed from human body to their animal form. At her continued silence, he sighed. "Well, he deserved to die, so good job."

He wholeheartedly approved of her brand of justice. Hopefully Aurora wouldn't be too disappointed, but he could, at least, guarantee that the authorities learned the truth about Drayger. The photo album of his victims sat on the dresser, obscene in its blatant spot out in the open, and it wouldn't be difficult for the cops to figure out where his dungeons were once they knew what they were looking for.

The female's voice trembled as she spoke. "You...you know what he was?"

"I know far too much about what he was." He frowned. "How do *you* know? Who are you?"

She took the photo album off the dresser, handling it as if it were a live grenade as she flipped it open and handed it to him. His gut dropped to his feet at the pictures of a dead, dismembered woman who was the spitting image of the female in front of him.

And now he knew why she looked familiar.

"Oh, damn," he said roughly, slamming the book closed. "Was Lexi your twin sister?"

"No," she said, her voice a low, tortured growl. "*I'm* Lexi. He tortured and killed me." She grabbed one of Drayger's green and yellow Oregon Duck T-shirts from off a hanger and slipped it on, covering herself all the way to mid-thigh. "I had nine lives. I'm down to six."

What the hell did someone say to that? He could only imagine how much it would suck to live through three deaths and remember them. And she had more to go. Poor female was going to need a lot of therapy.

Sirens sounded in the distance, growing louder. "I'm sorry," he said lamely. "But we'd better go. Can I take you somewhere?"

Her eyes narrowed, skepticism creeping into her posture, and he couldn't blame her. "I don't think so."

"I'm an angel," he said gently. "You can trust me. I can take you almost anywhere you want to go."

Her dubious snort was accompanied by further narrowing of her eyes until they were little more than slits. "Angels kill my kind, and call me a wuss, but I'm not ready to die again."

"I'm not that kind of angel." He wasn't sure what kind of angel he even was anymore. He might be *no* kind of angel soon enough.

But one thing he *was* sure of was that, angel or not, he was going to be a fucking great father.

She gestured to the deep laceration in her leg. "Are you familiar with Underworld General Hospital?"

"All too well," he muttered. "Let's go."

The sirens became deafening as he reached for her hand, but before he flashed them out of there, he saw movement out of the corner of his eye. He whipped his head around so fast a human would have suffered from whiplash. Drayger's head, there it was, sticking out from under the bed. And it was...collapsing. What the hell? His gaze flicked from body part to body part. His arms, legs, torso...all the parts were deflating like tires with no air.

"What's going on?" Lexi stared at the scene in horror. "I thought he was human."

"I thought so too." A sudden, terrifying thought popped into his head, and as he watched Drayger's remains become nothing but empty skins, he understood what was happening. "Oh, shit," he whispered. "Oh...*fuck*."

"What?" Lexi tugged on his arm. "Tell me!"

"Drayger wasn't human. He was a fucking bludgolem."

"A what?"

He wracked his brain for information he'd stored away since his first years of training, when he'd been required to learn about every type of known demon. Bludgolems were rare, so rare he'd never seen one, nor heard of anyone encountering one. But there were rumors. Lots of rumors.

"They're like viruses. They infect hosts, usually children. They spend years infecting the child's mind, and they're only released when the host dies."

"Released? So the bludgolem is still alive?"

"And looking for a new host."

"Another child?"

He shook his head. "According to legend, if they have unfinished business, they'll infect an adult, and they'll take over, using the person to finish whatever it is—" He broke off with a curse. "*Aurora.*"

"Who?"

He didn't bother replying. He grabbed Lexi's hand and flashed to Underworld General, dropped her off in the parking lot, and flashed back to Aurora's house.

The screams reached his ears before he'd even fully materialized.

Chapter Nineteen

The ward Aurora had set should have stopped the stranger from coming into her house. It hadn't even slowed him.

As she sprinted toward the front door, another scream of terror and pain lodged in her throat. Blood dripped to her hardwood floor from the stab wound in her arm. She shouldn't have investigated the noise in her bedroom. She should have trusted her instincts and run out of the house. Instead, she'd found the bastard climbing through her bedroom window.

Silver fire hadn't even slowed him.

Suddenly, there was a flash, and a dark-haired guy with a scythe popped into the living room, putting himself between her and the stranger.

"Not today, fucker," he snarled.

Her guardian? Had to be. He resembled Hawkyn too closely to be anything else.

And damn, but he had good timing.

Another flash, and Hawkyn was there, menace rolling off him in a tangible wave, both hands gripping swords. He cast her a reassuring smile, and then he was shoulder to shoulder with his brother, forming a wall she knew nothing would get through.

The air around them went icy and still, and she swore she could feel their desire to fight. This was what they'd been bred to do, and anticipation wrapped around them like armor.

The stranger attacked, and within seconds it was apparent that the man who looked like a skinhead was not entirely human. Sharp, needle-like teeth replaced the tame human grille, fingers morphed into wicked, raptor-like claws, and its screech threatened to shatter her eardrums.

"Maddox!" Hawkyn shouted. "Flank him!"

Hawkyn moved like a dancer, a deadly, lightning-fast dancer. His blades whirled as if they were in a blender, cutting and slicing as Maddox carved chunks out of the stranger with his scythe and with some sort of electrical ability that left thin, smoking gashes all over the demon's body.

The angels fought well together, completely in tandem, as if they'd practiced beforehand. But when the stranger got a powerful blow in, knocking Maddox into her corner table and lamp, the momentum took a nosedive, and suddenly Hawkyn launched into a wild battle that was going to destroy what remained of her living room.

Not that she cared. Right now her only fear was for Hawkyn and Maddox, and for the tiny life growing inside her.

She held her breath, waiting for the demon do go down, but it wasn't even slowing. Even when Maddox sent a dizzying volley of lightning, fireballs, and ice needles at him, the demon in a Nazi-tatted skin suit kept fighting. If anything, it seemed to gain strength from the weapons.

She was going to have a hell of a time explaining this to the insurance company.

Wait... It gained strength from weapons. Could a weapon *drain* it too?

"Hawkyn!" she yelled. "Over here!" She dove under her kitchen table, an ancient aluminum-legged thing that wouldn't protect her from jack shit, but would provide a little cover. Hopefully just enough.

Spinning, Hawkyn moved toward her, bringing the creature closer. When Maddox finally gave up trying to use his powers on the thing, he jumped back into the fray with his scythe and together, he and Hawkyn forced the demon to her.

Praying this worked, she grabbed the thing's foot and drew on his negative energy. Never before had she taken power from a demon, and the oily, ugly thread of current running through her made her want to puke.

It screeched in anger and tried to jerk away from her, but she held on with both hands, riding the thing like a rodeo bull as it kicked her around the room while trying to fend off Hawkyn and Maddox.

She hit the wall, furniture, and even Hawkyn once, but she refused to let go. The thing was slowing down now, growing sluggish, and the angels were doing more damage with each blow.

"We got it," Hawkyn yelled. "It's going down! Aurora, let go!"

Gladly. She released the thing and rolled against the wall, barely avoiding a vicious kick as the demon tried to get one more blow in before it collapsed, teeth gnashing.

Hawkyn lunged, bringing his sword down in a powerful arc that sliced the thing's head from its body in a single, powerful blow.

Then he was there, cradling her in his arms. "Aurora, honey? Are you okay?"

"I'm fine," she assured him. "I'm just going to be sore for a little while." She glanced over at the body Maddox was poking with his boot, presumably to make sure it was dead. "What is that thing? And why did it attack me?"

"It's Drayger."

Her gut clenched and she couldn't stop the shudder that wracked her body. And just kept wracking it. "W-what?"

"I've got you," he murmured, holding her tighter. "He can't hurt you now."

She knew that. If nothing else, she knew Hawkyn had her back, and gradually, surrounded by safety, she stopped shaking. "How...how is that Drayger?"

Hawkyn stroked her hair as he held her, his touch soothing and so gentle she wanted to cry. This big warrior was going to be so beautiful with an infant in those strong hands.

"When I got to his house," he said softly, "Drayger was dead. Someone killed him just before I got there. But that's when I figured out that he's a bludgolem. He was able to possess that human and use him as a vehicle to take revenge on you." He shook his head. "It was a suicide mission. When bludgolems infect someone that quickly, it burns them out. He was just hoping he could take you out with him."

She blew out a long, relieved breath, thankful that he and Maddox had shown up when they had. "Who killed him? The original Drayger, I mean."

"One of his victims. She wanted revenge."

"Someone else got away from him?"

"Long story," he said with a teasing smile. "I'll tell you after."

"After what?"

"After we get you a thorough exam at Underworld General."

Tilting her head up, she kissed him. "And after that?"

"After that, I give you my own thorough exam."

"Gag." Maddox shook his head. "I don't know what's going on here, but Hawk, you know the rules about Primori and Memitim, right?" He cursed. "Whatever." Turning to her, he waved. "Hey, I'm Maddox, by the way. You're not supposed to know about me, but apparently, according to Hawkyn, anyway, the rules are just rough guidelines." He shot Hawkyn a look that said they'd talk later. "I'm out of here."

In the blink of an eye, he was gone, but suddenly, in his place was a blinding white light, streaming into her house from nowhere, like an alien ship in a movie.

"Uh, Hawkyn?"

His expression was stony, hard, and a fresh wave of anxiety shivered through her. Couldn't they go more than five minutes without a crisis?

"I have to go." He stood, bringing her with him, and then he set her down carefully. "But I'll be back."

For some reason, she wasn't reassured. "Go where?"

"Heaven." He stared at the light, but it was impossible to tell what he was thinking. "The Memitim Council wants to see me."

No. Oh, no. "I don't want you to go." She gripped his forearm in desperation, as if she could hold him there forever. "I have a bad feeling..."

Shaking his head, he framed her face in his big hands and met her gaze. "This is kind of a non-optional thing. We can't run from the light. I'll come back. But listen to me, if, for some reason, I don't return, Maddox will take care of you."

"You said you're coming back!"

"That's the plan. I can't think of a reason I won't be back. But the Council has a way of getting creative with its punishments, so we'll see what happens. But know this, Aurora. You're Primori for a reason." He smiled, and pride thickened his voice. "The child you're carrying is special. I can feel it. No matter what, the world is going to be a better place because of us. Because of you. Everything will turn out the way it's supposed to."

She wanted to believe him. She could tell that he wanted to believe it too. But when he kissed her goodbye, too much doubt filled her mind. And when he stepped into the light, she couldn't help but fear that she'd seen him for the last time.

Chapter Twenty

Hawkyn's heart was heavy as he stepped out of the light and into a completely empty room. There was literally nothing but white nothingness. White nothingness and his mother, dressed in more white. At least her ruby red wings added some color.

"Hello, my son."

She really wanted to play the family card right now? Okay, he could do that. "Hey, Mom. So you drew the short straw, huh?"

"Short straw? Is that a humanism?"

And in those two short sentences, he truly understood why, until recently, Memitim had been raised by humans. Angels who rarely left the luxury of Heaven could never understand them.

"Yes, it's a humanism," he said as he looked around, marveling at all the nothing. "This isn't the Ascension chamber, is it? So I'm guessing I'm here for punishment, and you are the one who gets to deliver the sentence."

"This *is* most difficult," she said softly, and the first thread of *oh-shit* ran through his system.

What if he didn't make it back to Aurora? What if she really was left by herself to raise a half-angel child? And as much as he liked Maddox, the guy wasn't the most responsible angel who had ever existed.

"Tell me, Hawkyn. What rules have you broken?"

He snorted. There was no sense in lying, so at this point, he might as well go all in. "All of them, probably. So if I'm here to lose my Memitim status, can we just get it over with? I have somewhere to be."

"Yes," she mused. "With the mother of your child. How sweet."

"Says the person who tossed me away like garbage in a rainstorm."

Yeah, there was a little resentment there. It was stupid, probably, given that centuries had passed. But now that he had made a child, he couldn't understand how anyone could intentionally make a child to be given over, intentionally and knowingly, into harsh conditions.

He would protect his child—and its mother—with his life.

Centuries of anger spilled over at the thought, his abandonment issues rising to the surface like lake pollution after a storm.

"You know," he continued, because what the hell—if he was going to lose his angel status, he was going to make sure the Council knew exactly why it was bullshit. "Memitim deserve better than the kind of crap we've had to endure for eons, starting with the day we're born and abandoned in the worst conditions imaginable. We suffer only to be rescued from our situations and used as pawns in a game we aren't allowed to understand."

Ulnara's blond brows arched, but if she was annoyed by his tirade, it didn't show. "And what don't you understand?"

He nearly laughed. Where to even start…

"I want to know why we can't be told the reasons why the people we protect are Primori."

"And if you knew?"

"If we knew there was a good reason to protect evil people, then maybe it would be a little less soul-withering to watch them slaughter and torture and cause pain."

Clasping her delicate hands in front of her, she studied him with something he might have thought was affection if he didn't know any better. "Thousands of years ago, the very first Memitim were given that information." She sighed. "But we discovered that when they knew the future, they sometimes tried to change it. They always believed they could make bad things better. They didn't understand that real change comes from tragedy. It's how humans grow."

Okay, Hawkyn didn't like the rule, but he at least understood it. They could, however, make it more palatable and less "do it because I said so."

"Couldn't the same be said about angels?" he countered. "You people are stuck in the human dark ages, your rules and laws barely changing, while Memitim are moving forward because of human advancements in technology and science and social norms." He shook his head in frustration. "Can't you see what you're doing to us? We don't want to follow your rules anymore."

She tucked her hands behind her back and started to pace. Reminded him of himself, actually. "We're starting to see that." She looked over at him. "What would Memitim like to see changed?"

He stared. Was she serious? And was this why he'd been summoned? To brainstorm options to raise Memitim morale?

"Well?" she prompted.

Right. He ticked shit off his fingers. "First off, we'd love to have sex. Like, we'd really love it. Second, we need access to Primori records. Even if we can't know why our charges are special, it would be helpful to know their histories, especially if we're their first guardians or if their previous guardian didn't keep detailed notes." He'd been lucky with Drayger that Atticus had been so obsessive about record-keeping, much like himself. Some Memitim, like Journey, half-assed their notes while others took none at all. "It would be especially helpful if we can see, in real time, if our Primori have gone off track. Third, why the hell can't we have an occasional margarita? That's some serious bullshit right there. Fourth—"

"Okay." She held up her hand to cut him off. "I think that's enough."

Now that he was on a roll, he didn't want to stop. "It's not nearly enough," he said, more harshly than he intended. "But hey, I can submit the rest to you in writing." He snorted. "Except you guys never acknowledge anything we send you. That's another thing; maybe you could actually respond to our summons? Reza waited at the Summoning Stone for three full days after sending a request, and she never did hear from you. That's unacceptable. If this were a human business, you'd go under within a year."

Suddenly, his tongue froze and his lips stopped moving. Ulnara smiled. "That's better. When I tell you enough, it means enough." She flicked her fingers, and his oral bits started functioning again. "Perhaps you'd like to know why you're here?"

No shit. "That'd be great."

She ruffled her wings, the sound whispering through the great empty space. "You impregnated a Wytch."

Here we go. Now they were getting down to it. "Yeah, and I don't know how it even happened. I mean, aside from the obvious. I shouldn't be fertile."

"I have no idea why you are fertile," she said. "My job doesn't usually focus on how things happen. I'm more concerned with the results." She studied him with hawklike eyes. "But it *is* curious. Did you eat or drink anything that could have altered your physiology? Has anyone cast a spell—or a curse—on you?"

"Of course not. I—" Oh, shit. The day with Darien. He'd spilled a drop of his mystery potion into Hawkyn's wound. That had to have been it. Darien had said the elixir had unpredictable results, but holy shitmonkeys, fertility was one hell of a side effect. "Yeah, I think I figured it out."

"It doesn't matter," she said with a dismissive wave of her hand. "It was meant to be. All of it. That's why your Primori's Fate Line didn't change when you tried to interfere with Aurora's abduction or when you rescued her. It was supposed to happen." Shockwaves pummeled him in almost physical blows. *He* had been part of the historical grand plan? "That said, we have to punish you even though everything you did was according to plan."

What kind of bullshit was that? "I don't understand," he ground out.

"Well, how could you? You're a mere earthbound Memitim." She adjusted her robes. Why, he didn't know. They looked the same as they had before she adjusted the folds. Still fold-y. "You're not going to Ascend. But you're not remaining as you were. We've created a position just for you."

"A...position?" He swallowed the lump of disbelief in his throat. They weren't going to expel him from the Memitim Order? He was getting *promoted*?

"In part, you can thank your father for that. He's been a supreme pain in the ass, and it's become clear that we need a closer relationship. So you are going to be the liaison between the Council and Sheoul-gra. You'll make the Council more accessible to Azagoth and your siblings, and you'll help advise us to make policy based on Memitim needs."

Holy shit. *Holy shit*! All his life, all he'd wanted was to be on the Council so he could be a leader for his un-Ascended brethren, making life easier for them, supporting them, making sure they were happy and functional. A job as a liaison would be even better, allowing him to still be with his earthbound siblings while advising the Council.

"We've heard you, Hawkyn." She smiled wryly. "How could we not? You send missives on a weekly basis."

"So you really do get those?" he asked, incredulous. "I assumed they get tossed out with the Heavenly trash."

"We got every one of them. Including the ones in which you call us doddering fools who are out of touch with reality." She sniffed haughtily. "We're not doddering or fools, but we are, perhaps, a little out of touch with reality."

"A little?"

"Watch it," she warned. "The other Council members were skeptical of this plan. I stood up for you. I can stand down." She flapped her wings in irritation, and he wondered how close he was to losing this. He should probably be a little more respectful.

Nah.

"When does this become effective?"

"Right now."

Powerful waves of tingly energy rolled over him, rushing through his veins like a drug, filling him with new knowledge, new abilities, and, he was thrilled to find out, new wings. Cranking his head, he took them in, shocked to see that they resembled his old ones. Like his shadow wings, these were transparent, smoke-colored. But they were bigger, and they glittered, catching the white light like a disco ball.

"There are no feathers," he said thickly, his voice heavy with emotion. "But they're beautiful."

"They are as unique as you are, my son."

She smiled, and in that moment, he felt her affection surround him. Suddenly, hundreds of years of feeling as if he hadn't mattered at all to the people who conceived him vanished, and he got it. He truly got it. He'd been raised by humans, so he'd applied human values to his situation and had been unable to fully understand angelic ways. That didn't mean he liked the way angels did things, but he was at peace with it now.

And it was all because of Aurora.

He flapped his wings, closing his eyes as the breeze they made ruffled his hair and caressed his skin. He couldn't wait to show her.

"What does this all of this mean for me now?"

When he opened his eyes, Ulnara was still smiling. "As an Un-

Ascended Memitim, you don't have access to all of Heaven, but you will be able to move around the Memitim compound and embassy freely. You can reside in Sheoul-gra or the earthly realm for now. When the time for the Final Battle comes, you'll be granted full Ascension."

"What about Aurora? I won't give her up, even if she's Primori."

She shrugged. "She won't be Primori for long. Her status will shift to the child she carries once it's born. Be with her, Hawkyn. Should you choose to mate her, your eternal lifespan will be hers. Either way, I should like to meet my grandchild one day."

Stunned, he barely managed a raspy, "Of course."

"I hope you aren't too disappointed in our decision."

Disappointed? This...this was more than he'd ever hoped for. This was far better than Ascending, but he couldn't let them know that. The Memitim Council thought this was a compromise between punishment and Ascension, and if they knew this was the ultimate reward, he'd lose some bargaining power.

Bargaining power he was going to use right now.

"Well, you're saying I have to spend the next nine-plus centuries working as an Ascended angel but without all the benefits, right?" He affected a troubled expression. "Can we at least start this off with an olive branch between Azagoth and the Council? He's pretty pissed off at me, and if I can negotiate a deal, it'll go a long way toward making my position legitimate in the eyes of my siblings and my father."

She appeared to consider his BS, and he was shocked when she nodded. "What is this olive branch you want us to extend to the bastard?"

He grinned. "You're not going to like it."

She didn't. But he got it anyway.

Chapter Twenty-One

Hawkyn held Aurora's hand tight as they materialized in Sheoul-gra. As Primori, she wasn't supposed to be here, but he'd gotten permission from the Council to break that rule, just this once.

They'd been remarkably cool about it. Maybe they were loosening up already.

"Are you sure your father is going to be okay with us being here?" she asked as they stepped off the landing pad.

He honestly wasn't sure, but he didn't want her to worry. "He'll be fine. He's going to have to get used to my presence no matter what, now that I'm the liaison between him and the Council."

They strode through the courtyard and up the giant staircase leading to Azagoth's mansion, and as they entered, Emerico came out.

Hawkyn had a heartbeat to decide if he wanted to be nice…or if he wanted to rip Rico's lungs out of his rib cage the way Hawkyn's shadow wings had been torn out of his.

In the next heartbeat, he had his half-brother up against the side of the building, his forearm across his throat. Nice it was. But only because Aurora didn't need to see any more of Hawk's violent side.

"You piece of shit," he said, keeping his voice level. "You ratted me out to the Council."

"Yeah, I did."

Hawkyn had to hand it to the guy. He was a weasel, but he was pretty open about it. "I don't need to ask why, but I want to know what you got out of it."

Rico's grin was all fang. "A clean slate. All my sins gone. Sorry, man, but I had a couple of wing-shrivelers in my past. I needed something juicy to get them removed."

As much as Hawkyn hated the answer, he understood it. Ascension was the goal of every Memitim, and when failure meant spending an eternity in the human realm—or worse, it was every angel for himself.

That was something else Hawkyn planned to change.

"You're a bastard," Hawkyn growled as he shoved away from Rico. "Stay away me, brother. And if you fuck with anyone I care about, you'll deal with me." He flared his wings, sending a message of strength his brother would understand. Hawkyn hadn't played around with his new powers yet, but he already knew that they were far more extensive and powerful than anything Rico could even begin to comprehend.

Rico nodded, a deep dip of his head, and scurried away like the rat he was.

"I'm sorry you had to deal with that," Aurora said as he grasped her hand again and guided her through the mansion on the way to Azagoth's office. "Are you okay? I can't imagine my own brother betraying me."

"I'm okay." He smiled down at her. "Really. I've been dealing with shithead siblings for centuries. Rico is a product of his human upbringing and Memitim rules that pit us against one another. But shit's going to change, so that's all that matters."

They stopped at the door to Azagoth's office, and he had to tamp down butterflies as he knocked.

A moment later, the office door swung open, and they stepped inside. Azagoth and Lilliana were sitting in the two big leather chairs near the fire. She looked curious, and Hawkyn couldn't tell what the hell his father was thinking. His expression was a mask, his eyes utterly flat. The guy would slay it at a poker tournament.

"I heard you got a promotion," Azagoth said, his voice as flat as his eyes.

Word traveled fast. Hawkyn had gone straight from the Memitim complex to Aurora's place, where she'd been busy cleaning up after the battle had practically destroyed her house. Maddox, at least, had taken the human's body away, the empty, broken shell left behind after the bludgolem died.

They'd showered, made love, eaten, made love again, and now he was ready to face his father after their blowout.

"I'm officially the liaison between Sheoul-gra and the Council," Hawkyn said. "But I can't do my job if I'm not welcome here."

Finally, there was a chink in Azagoth's non-expressive armor. Just a slight widening of his eyes, but it was there. For a moment.

"Why would you not be welcome here? I told you it was your choice."

"You didn't try to talk me out of it," Hawkyn pointed out. "You didn't give a shit."

Azagoth laughed. "If I didn't give a shit, I wouldn't have given you a choice at all. Do you think I'm shy about kicking people out of my realm?"

"He's not. He's really, really not." Lilliana smiled. "Congratulations, Hawkyn. You'll have to tell us how it happened. From what I understand, the Council created a position and a status for you. That's...incredible."

It was. Made him wonder what role the child Aurora carried would play in the future, if Hawkyn was being rewarded for his own role in conceiving it.

"I have more incredible news," he said, barely able to contain his excitement. This was big. Bigger than a relaxing of the rules allowing them to drink. He handed Azagoth a scroll.

Azagoth broke the seal and started to unroll it. "What is it?"

"The first batch of names and information you need to find your sons and daughters who are still in the human world."

Hawkyn doubted that anyone had ever seen Azagoth as shocked as he was at that moment. The parchment shook as he stared down at it, and when Lilliana reached over to take his hand, he hauled her against him. He just held her like that for a long time, his gaze glued to the scroll, his chest heaving against Lilliana's cheek.

"I don't..." He cleared his throat and looked up at Hawkyn. "I don't know what to say."

"That's a first," Lilliana muttered, but she was smiling, and the gratitude in her eyes as she nodded her thanks at Hawkyn made this even better.

He hadn't known how she'd react. After all, a lot of small children, in-your-face reminders of her mate's unions with other females, were going to be invading her territory.

He should have known Lilliana would be happy for her mate.

Slowly, as if emotions were weighing him down, Azagoth came over to Hawkyn.

"Thank you," he said roughly. "This...is incredible."

"Don't take this the wrong way," Hawkyn said, "but I'm surprised this was so important to you. You barely acknowledge our existence most of the time. Why bring in even more of us?"

Azagoth glanced over at Lilliana, who smiled reassuringly. When he turned back to Hawkyn, there was warmth in his gaze. Not hot flames of malevolence, but genuine, warm emotion.

"My life was devoid of meaning for a long time," Azagoth said. "I had a duty, but not a life. Lilliana brought life to me, and my sons and daughters have brought even more. I thought I didn't have room for it all, but I do. I just have to remember not to fight it."

Hawkyn had no idea what that meant, but Lilliana did, and even through the joy in her expression, he thought he saw a flicker of worry. But maybe that was just his imagination.

"I understand Azagoth has a new grandchild on the way?" Lilliana said, coming to her feet. "Congratulations, you two. I'm guessing there's a lot for you to work out now."

Aurora nodded vehemently. They still had to figure out where they were going to live while Aurora's house was being repaired, they had baby plans to make, and before the baby came, they had to get to know each other even more.

He was going to enjoy every second he spent learning about her—inside and out.

"I'm happy for you," Azagoth said, and in a shocking move, he wrapped his arm around Hawkyn's neck and hauled him in for a brief, powerful hug. "And I'm proud of you."

Hawkyn's eyes stung. He'd never had a parent. Even after he'd moved here, Azagoth had been less a father and more a dictator. His affection had been fleeting, as intangible as a ghost. He'd felt it now and then, but in an instant it would be gone, and Hawk would wonder if it had truly been there at all.

This time, there was no doubt.

For the first time in his life, he had no doubts about anything. For the moment, life was perfect.

Chapter Twenty-Two

Finally something had gone his way. Azagoth was going to have all his young children here, delivered out of their human hells and raised with brothers and sisters who shared similar experiences. His kids would be happy, well cared for, and he planned to play an active role in their upbringing.

He never would have imagined that any of this could happen. Hell, he hadn't wanted it to happen. Not for thousands of years. Lilliana had changed him, and it was absolutely for the better. Sure, there was the downside of experiencing things like hurt and guilt, but love was worth it.

Lilliana was worth it.

He swept into the bedroom, prepared to sweep her into his arms and show her what she meant to him. He was going to spend a full day doing nothing but spoiling her. Feeding her the best food. Bathing her in a tub full of Champagne. Tending to her every want and need.

But the second he stepped across the threshold, he knew something was wrong.

Terror formed like a hot coal in his belly, turning to downright panic when he saw the note on his pillow.

His hand shook as he picked it up the lavender-scented paper, and his eyes grew blurry as he read his mate's flowing script.

My Love,

You are my world. You know that. I've never been happier than I have been since I met you, and you've said the same about me. But right now I think we're both overwhelmed by the changes in our lives and the emotions those changes have unearthed. You have so many children you need to get to know and to understand, and you need to do it on your own. I can't help anymore, not when my presence is causing confusion.

As for myself, you know I love your sons and daughters. Well, I love many of them. Others I'm still getting to know. Still others...well, there are a few who vex me and a couple who actively despise me, and I'm not overly fond of them either. No matter what, though, I want your family around us, and I'm excited for all the little ones who will be saved from miserable lives in the human world and who will be brought to Sheoul-gra to know their siblings and father.

You need to handle it yourself. You'll be fine. I know you will.

I won't be gone long, I don't think, but I promise, I'll be back.

I love you.

Lilliana

The letter slipped from Azagoth's numb fingers. He watched it float to the floor as he sank to his knees, his legs unable to support the weight of his grief.

Lilliana had left him. He didn't know how she'd done it, given that she'd been all but locked inside Sheoul-gra by archangels, but somehow, she'd escaped.

She said it was temporary, and he believed her. So as much as he wanted to scream, to throw Sheoul-gra into chaos, he had to resist. He had to justify her faith in him.

He'd welcome his new children and make things right with the ones already living here.

And then he'd fight like hell to get Lilliana back and to make sure she never left again.

Chapter Twenty-Three

It had been almost a month since Aurora's house had been nearly destroyed by two Memitim angels and a bludgolem, and today was the day she and Hawkyn could finally move in. She'd loved staying with his sister Idess and her mate, Lore, and their son, Mace, while contractors put her house back together, but it was way past time to have some privacy.

"I'll just be happy to not hear them at all hours of the day," Hawkyn had grumbled as they were packing. "Sex demons, man. How does Idess handle it?"

Aurora had promptly stuck her hand down his pants. "Are you saying I could ever wear you out?"

"Not a chance," he'd said, returning the favor.

Idess and Lore were probably tired of hearing them, too.

Hawkyn dumped their bags on the new living room floor and looked around. Furniture would be there this afternoon, making the already small space even smaller. They'd discussed moving, but she loved this place, and until the baby was born, she wanted to be comfortable and stable. Hawk had agreed, understanding that she'd been through a lot, with more to come, and this was home.

It was going to be even more of a home with Hawkyn in it.

"I think we should check out the bedroom," he said. "Make sure it's up to par."

She frowned. "The bedroom wasn't damaged."

He waggled his brow, and her knees went weak. "Wanna do some damage?"

Oh, yes. Yes, she did. She wanted to do a *lot* of damage. "Are we talking wrecking ball damage, or sledgehammer to the studs kind of damage?"

Flashing to her, he swept her up and hauled her to the bedroom. "Sledgehammer. You're pregnant. But after the baby... I'll get out the wrecking balls."

She laughed and wedged her hand between their bodies so she could cup him through his jeans. "I think I'll be the one wrecking balls."

His groan vibrated every erogenous zone as he laid her out on the bed, and by the time he'd stripped her of every scrap of clothing and spread her out on the comforter, she was on fire.

"Don't move," he told her in a commanding voice that she didn't dare disobey. Hell, no. She wasn't going to risk screwing up whatever he had planned for her.

It was funny how she had more sexual experience than he did, and yet he had an erotic instinct that couldn't be taught or learned. He could read her every breath, every shiver, every twitch of her muscles. He knew what she wanted and when. How fast, how hard, how dirty.

She watched him strip, loving how his supple bronze skin rippled over powerful muscles that moved with fluid grace and machine-like efficiency. Every time he removed an article of clothing, he did something to her. His T-shirt earned her a tender peck on the lips. His boots a lingering kiss on the neck. He sucked her nipples into his mouth, laving them with attention after he tossed his socks aside.

Soon, he was left only in jeans, no underwear, and her body grew liquid with anticipation. As he worked his fly with nimble fingers, she squirmed, whimpering when his hand went still and he shook his head.

"I told you not to move."

"But—"

"Nope." He lifted his hands, holding them up so they weren't doing what they were supposed to be doing, which was either get him naked or get her off. "Spread your legs. Wider. There you go. I want to see all of you."

She growled with frustration. "You're so cruel."

His casual shrug would have made her laugh if her entire body wasn't throbbing with desire right now. "I do take after my father in some ways, I guess."

Man, she loved that he was able to speak about Azagoth with easy affection now. Hawkyn's job required him to work closely with his father, and Azagoth had been making real efforts to include not only Hawkyn, but all of his children, in Gra business. Before, the Memitim had only lived there, and Azagoth had been their landlord. Now Azagoth was trying to make Sheoul-gra a home.

Of course, it wasn't easy. Azagoth was famous for not being one to share, for making bargains that overwhelmingly benefitted him, and for being extremely distrustful. With Lilliana "on vacation," he'd been moody, but Hawkyn said the moods were more often good ones than bad ones now.

But even on the bad days that made Hawkyn moody as well, he'd come to her, and she'd taken it all away. Sometimes she'd knead away his tension with a massage that always turned hot, and other times he'd feed from her. Gently. Tenderly. Taking just enough from her to energize them both.

"Can we not talk about your father and instead talk about how you're going to take your pants off?" she asked as she gripped the mattress hard to keep her hands from ripping the rest of his clothes off herself.

"You want me to talk about taking off my pants?" He reached down and popped a button, revealing the plum-ripe head of his erection. "Wouldn't you rather I talk about what I'm going to do to you after I take them off?"

"Oh, yes," she breathed. "Tell me."

He freed another button, exposing a mouthwatering length of his dusky shaft. "I'm going to lick you everywhere, but I'm not going to tease you." Another button. More shaft and more mouth watering. "I'm going to dive right between your legs and fill you with my tongue. I'm going to do that thing you like, you know, when I curl my tongue when it's deep inside and hit you in that place that makes you come over and over."

Oh, God, she was practically there already. Anticipation made her core clench and her breasts ache. She couldn't keep her body still, her hips grinding on the mattress, her pelvis tilting up, inviting him to hurry.

"That's it," he murmured in a taut, husky voice. "Lift your knees. Dig your heels into the mattress so I can see all of you."

Cheeks burning with both lust and a bit of shy inhibition, she did what he wanted, loving how his eyes went half-lidded and hotly possessive, and his chest heaved with a shuddering breath.

"That's it, baby." He popped the last button, freeing his straining erection.

He didn't even wait to shove down his pants. He did exactly what he'd said he'd do and dove between her legs, thrusting his tongue inside her. A shout of ecstasy tore from her throat as he pressed the tip of his tongue against that spot he'd spoken of, sending her instantly, wildly, into her first orgasm.

He gripped her hips as he worked her through it, licking and sucking, and before the first one ended, another queued up right behind it.

"You taste so good," he moaned against her, and the vibrations triggered yet another blinding climax.

She felt as though she were drowning in pleasure, like there was nothing around her except Hawkyn. Never had she been so happy. Never had she felt so cherished. And when he reared up and entered her in one smooth, almost violent motion, she realized she'd never been so freaking *alive.*

"You're gorgeous," he purred before his mouth found hers in a hot, urgent kiss.

He ground against her, his hips churning between her legs, and she lost herself to the passion he so easily brought out in her. Electric strikes of sensation sizzled at the tip of every nerve ending, making her lose control. She arched upward, spreading her legs even wider, demanding every inch he could give her.

A rumble of approval echoed in his chest and throat as he kissed a path across her cheek and changed up the rhythm of his thrusts, keeping her off balance, forcing her to concentrate on every delicious stroke. Good Lord, she burned for him, couldn't get enough. She quivered with the need to come, but he kept her right on the edge with his incredible ability to adjust and adapt his touch, his thrusts, his hot breath as it fanned over her ear.

Dragging her hands down his back, she caressed every muscle, massaging with her fingers as she worked her way to his buttocks. She gripped him firmly, digging in as she locked her legs around his and met his thrusts with eager ones of her own. When her nails scored him, he went crazy, pumping into her in a frenzy. The slick, hot friction became too much, and she screamed his name as she finally went over the edge.

He went taut, his body straining, his head rocked back in a portrait of male ecstasy as he came. He jerked, his hot seed splashing inside her, stimulating her sensitive tissues beyond what she could handle, and yet another orgasm launched her into heights she wasn't sure she could come down from.

Somehow, she did come down. She could barely move, her limbs tangled with his, his heavy weight pinning her to the mattress. He shifted onto his side and pulled her on top of him so she could breathe, and they lay that way for a long time, just taking in the moment. And each other.

"Oh," she finally said with a yawn, "did I tell you my parents and brother will be here tomorrow?"

"What?" Hawkyn jackknifed up, practically throwing her off of him. "Tomorrow? I thought you said next week."

"I did. Last week." She giggled at the panic in his expression. He really did want to make a good impression. Hawkyn, an angel with powers her family couldn't comprehend, was worried about meeting her parents and brother.

"What if they hate me?"

Gently, she took his hand in hers. "What if they do? It won't change anything." She kissed his knuckles. "But they won't. I mean, come on. I landed an *angel*. I'm like, a celebrity in the Wytch community now. Besides, unless my brother accidentally knocks someone up, he's never going to get married and give them grandchildren." She winked. "So that makes me the one they can't piss off."

Laughing, he twisted around and took her back down to the mattress. As she lay back on the pillow, he covered her body with his and propped himself up on his elbows above her. Behind him, his exquisite wings spread out and lowered to wrap them in a cocoon of intimacy, an angel's embrace that was more than affectionate. It was a promise, a vow, and it was *everything*.

His eyes gleamed with a wicked spark that lit her up again. She was always quick to ignite around him. She would always be tinder to his flame.

"I love you," he whispered, and her eyes stung.

This was the first time he'd said that. And when she said it back, it might have been the first time she'd spoken those words out loud, but she knew, without a doubt, that the love had been there almost from the beginning.

And this *was* a beginning. The beautiful thing was that, thanks to their eternal lives, she didn't have to worry about an ending. At least, not the bad kind.

Because as Hawkyn eased himself inside her, she was counting on having many, many happy endings.

* * * *

Also from 1001 Dark Nights and Larissa Ione, discover Azagoth, Hades, Z, and Razr.

Sign up for the 1001 Dark Nights Newsletter
and be entered to win a Tiffany Key necklace.

There's a contest every month!

Go to www.1001DarkNights.com to subscribe.

As a bonus, all subscribers will receive a free copy of
Discovery Bundle Three
Featuring stories by
Sidney Bristol, Darcy Burke, T. Gephart
Stacey Kennedy, Adriana Locke
JB Salsbury, and Erika Wilde

Discover 1001 Dark Nights Collection Five

Go to www.1001DarkNights.com for more information.

BLAZE ERUPTING by Rebecca Zanetti
Scorpius Syndrome/A Brigade Novella

ROUGH RIDE by Kristen Ashley
A Chaos Novella

HAWKYN by Larissa Ione
A Demonica Underworld Novella

RIDE DIRTY by Laura Kaye
A Raven Riders Novella

ROME'S CHANCE by Joanna Wylde
A Reapers MC Novella

THE MARRIAGE ARRANGEMENT by Jennifer Probst
A Marriage to a Billionaire Novella

SURRENDER by Elisabeth Naughton
A House of Sin Novella

INKED NIGHT by Carrie Ann Ryan
A Montgomery Ink Novella

ENVY by Rachel Van Dyken
An Eagle Elite Novella

PROTECTED by Lexi Blake
A Masters and Mercenaries Novella

THE PRINCE by Jennifer L. Armentrout
A Wicked Novella

PLEASE ME by J. Kenner
A Stark Ever After Novella

WOUND TIGHT by Lorelei James
A Rough Riders/Blacktop Cowboys Novella®

STRONG by Kylie Scott
A Stage Dive Novella

DRAGON NIGHT by Donna Grant
A Dark Kings Novella

TEMPTING BROOKE by Kristen Proby
A Big Sky Novella

HAUNTED BE THE HOLIDAYS by Heather Graham
A Krewe of Hunters Novella

CONTROL by K. Bromberg
An Everyday Heroes Novella

HUNKY HEARTBREAKER by Kendall Ryan
A Whiskey Kisses Novella

THE DARKEST CAPTIVE by Gena Showalter
A Lords of the Underworld Novella

Discover 1001 Dark Nights Collection One

Go to www.1001DarkNights.com for more information.

FOREVER WICKED by Shayla Black
CRIMSON TWILIGHT by Heather Graham
CAPTURED IN SURRENDER by Liliana Hart
SILENT BITE: A SCANGUARDS WEDDING by Tina Folsom
DUNGEON GAMES by Lexi Blake
AZAGOTH by Larissa Ione
NEED YOU NOW by Lisa Renee Jones
SHOW ME, BABY by Cherise Sinclair
ROPED IN by Lorelei James
TEMPTED BY MIDNIGHT by Lara Adrian
THE FLAME by Christopher Rice
CARESS OF DARKNESS by Julie Kenner

Also from 1001 Dark Nights

TAME ME by J. Kenner

Discover 1001 Dark Nights Collection Two

Go to www.1001DarkNights.com for more information.

WICKED WOLF by Carrie Ann Ryan
WHEN IRISH EYES ARE HAUNTING by Heather Graham
EASY WITH YOU by Kristen Proby
MASTER OF FREEDOM by Cherise Sinclair
CARESS OF PLEASURE by Julie Kenner
ADORED by Lexi Blake
HADES by Larissa Ione
RAVAGED by Elisabeth Naughton
DREAM OF YOU by Jennifer L. Armentrout
STRIPPED DOWN by Lorelei James
RAGE/KILLIAN by Alexandra Ivy/Laura Wright
DRAGON KING by Donna Grant
PURE WICKED by Shayla Black
HARD AS STEEL by Laura Kaye
STROKE OF MIDNIGHT by Lara Adrian
ALL HALLOWS EVE by Heather Graham
KISS THE FLAME by Christopher Rice
DARING HER LOVE by Melissa Foster
TEASED by Rebecca Zanetti
THE PROMISE OF SURRENDER by Liliana Hart

Also from 1001 Dark Nights

THE SURRENDER GATE By Christopher Rice
SERVICING THE TARGET By Cherise Sinclair

Discover 1001 Dark Nights Collection Three

Go to www.1001DarkNights.com for more information.

Discover 1001 Dark Nights Collection Four

Go to www.1001DarkNights.com for more information.

ROCK CHICK REAWAKENING by Kristen Ashley
ADORING INK by Carrie Ann Ryan
SWEET RIVALRY by K. Bromberg
SHADE'S LADY by Joanna Wylde
RAZR by Larissa Ione
ARRANGED by Lexi Blake
TANGLED by Rebecca Zanetti
HOLD ME by J. Kenner
SOMEHOW, SOME WAY by Jennifer Probst
TOO CLOSE TO CALL by Tessa Bailey
HUNTED by Elisabeth Naughton
EYES ON YOU by Laura Kaye
BLADE by Alexandra Ivy/Laura Wright
DRAGON BURN by Donna Grant
TRIPPED OUT by Lorelei James
STUD FINDER by Lauren Blakely
MIDNIGHT UNLEASHED by Lara Adrian
HALLOW BE THE HAUNT by Heather Graham
DIRTY FILTHY FIX by Laurelin Paige
THE BED MATE by Kendall Ryan
PRINCE ROMAN by CD Reiss
NO RESERVATIONS by Kristen Proby
DAWN OF SURRENDER by Liliana Hart

Also from 1001 Dark Nights

Tempt Me by J. Kenner

Her Guardian Angel

By Larissa Ione

A Demonica Underworld/Masters and Mercenaries Novella

Coming April 10, 2018

After a difficult childhood and a turbulent stint in the military, Declan Burke finally got his act together. Now he's a battle-hardened professional bodyguard who takes his job at McKay-Taggart seriously and his playtime – and his play*mates* – just as seriously. One thing he never does, however, is mix business with pleasure. But when the mysterious, gorgeous Suzanne D'Angelo needs his protection from a stalker, his desire for her burns out of control, tempting him to break all the rules…even as he's drawn into a dark, dangerous world he didn't know existed.

Suzanne is an earthbound angel on her critical first mission: protecting Declan from an emerging supernatural threat at all costs. To keep him close, she hires him as her bodyguard. It doesn't take long for her to realize that she's in over her head, defenseless against this devastatingly sexy human who makes her crave his forbidden touch.

Together they'll have to draw on every ounce of their collective training to resist each other as the enemy closes in, but soon it becomes apparent that nothing could have prepared them for the menace to their lives…or their hearts.

* * * *

Declan was at the end of his rope. In three days he hadn't found a reason for the lack of video showing Suzanne leaving the house and Hawkyn coming inside the house, and even more baffling, the doors and windows, which registered every instance of opening and closing, hadn't recorded anything during those times, either.

Why Suzanne would lie, he didn't know. And truth be told, he didn't think she was lying. But unless someone tampered with the evidence, there was no other explanation. But *why* would someone tamper with the evidence? Besides, McKay-Taggart's best techies confirmed that no tampering had taken place.

Something wasn't right about this entire situation, and he was about to get to the bottom of all of Suzanne's secrets, one way or another.

He stopped at the door beneath the stairs and tested the knob. It was as locked as it had been every time he'd tried, which was at least twice a day. And yet, Suzanne was able to turn the knob with no trouble.

Had to be some sort of advanced touch-sensor technology. But when he asked, she just shrugged and claimed to know nothing about it.

Yeah, something *definitely* wasn't right.

"So what are we doing in here?" she asked. "Looking for a secret door behind the...what is that thing?"

"It's a bondage horse." An exquisite one, in fact. The four legs were wooden, but the rest was padded and covered in leather, and the attachment on one end that looked like ancient punishment stocks, was worn but in good shape.

"Okay..." She stood there, looking confused and delectable in her blue and yellow sundress.

"Come here, Suzanne."

"What?"

"I said, come here."

She swallowed, the delicate muscles in her throat rippling, and he had a sudden urge to nibble his way along each one. Sure, he was disappointed in the way she'd treated him the other day in the security office, and he knew she was keeping something from him, but he also wanted to fuck her in the worst way.

Angry sex was still sex.

But that wasn't what this about. Not entirely, anyway.

"Why?" she asked.

"Do you trust me?"

She didn't hesitate. "Yes."

"Do you really?" He gestured to the bondage horse and stocks. "So if I cuff you to this, you would trust me not to hurt you."

Her chin came up, and her eyes sparked with determination. "Absolutely. But why do you want to do that?"

"Because *I* don't trust *you*, and that's a problem."

She jammed her fists on her hips. "You really think you can

torture me into telling you what you want to hear?"

"Yes…and no." He snagged two sets of handcuffs from where they hung on the wall. "This is going to be an exercise in trust, Suzanne. For everything you tell me, I'll tell you something. That's how it works."

For a moment she stared at the handcuffs, and then she squared her shoulders and marched over to the bondage horse. "Go ahead. You'll see that I'm not hiding anything."

Smirking, she held out her wrists to him, almost taunting him.

She was going to learn a lesson about that.

Without warning, he moved on her, slipping the cuffs on her wrists even as he maneuvered her body, angling her over the bench so she was lying on her belly, arms outstretched, her legs spread and her feet barely touching the floor. The fabric of her dress was stretched tight around her calves, so after he secured the cuffs to the stocks, he hiked the dress up to her hips.

He wasn't counting on the sight of her creamy, toned thighs and the pink silk panties that barely covered her tight round ass to grab him right by the cock. An instant erection strained at his fly, the impatient bastard.

"W—what are you doing?" She tried to look back at him, but her position didn't allow much movement.

"You safe word is…halo." He wasn't sure why that word popped into his head, but it seemed to fit both Suzanne and his stupid angel wing tattoo. "If you want me to stop at any time, say it."

"Stop…what, exactly?"

He slapped her ass, just a light one, and the sound echoed off the walls. "Shh. I'm asking the questions."

"But—"

He slapped her again, a little harder, and a rosy blush began to bloom on her right cheek.

"I ask the questions," he repeated. "I told you that's how this works." He pitched his voice low, quiet with an edge of command. "Understood?"

Irritation put color in her cheeks and a hot flare in her eyes, but she nodded.

"Good girl." In reward, he cupped her bottom, feeling the heat from the spanks in his palm, and used his thumb to stroke her inner thigh. She trembled when his thumb brushed the fabric of her panties, and when he added pressure, she squirmed.

"Now, tell me if there's a secret entrance to this house." He slipped his finger beneath the fabric and used the tip to caress, every so lightly the smooth, plump flesh between her legs.

"There's not," she blurted. "I told you."

He deepened his touch, adding more pressure and easing his finger inward, so he was stroking the seam of her labia. She went utterly still, but her breaths came in small bursts that shook the bench.

"Are you sure?"

"Well…there could be." She broke off on a moan and when she spoke again, her throaty voice had gone even lower. "But if there is, I don't know about it. Like this room."

Dammit, he believed her. Gently, he dipped his finger between her folds and nearly groaned at the silky moisture he found.

"Okay," he murmured. "Now I have to tell you something."

"Your tattoo," she blurted breathlessly. "I want to know about that."

Reflexively, he jerked his hand away. He didn't want to talk about his fucking tattoo. "First of all," he said, as he pinched the tender area he'd spanked, "you don't get to ask the questions." He brought his hand down on the spot he'd just pinched, and she hissed even as her lovely ass, framed by all that flowing fabric from her dress, rose as much as she could manage to meet his palm. "Second, my tattoo is off the table."

He swore she growled. "Then this is about trust, is it? If so, you need to give me something you don't want to give up."

As right as she was, he didn't want to hear it. This time, he pinched her between the legs. Not enough to hurt, but enough to startle her into making a squeal of both surprise and outrage. But when he began to pet her there, easing the throb he knew she was feeling, she moaned.

"Tell you what," he said softly. "You tell me who you *really* are, and I'll tell you what you want to know."

About Larissa Ione

Air Force veteran Larissa Ione traded in a career as a meteorologist to pursue her passion of writing. She has since published dozens of books, hit several bestseller lists, including the New York Times and USA Today, and has been nominated for a RITA award. She now spends her days in pajamas with her computer, strong coffee, and fictional worlds. She believes in celebrating everything, and would never be caught without a bottle of Champagne chilling in the fridge…just in case. After a dozen moves all over the country with her now-retired U.S. Coast Guard spouse, she is now settled in Wisconsin with her husband, her teenage son, a rescue cat named Vegas, and her very own hellhounds, a King Shepherd named Hexe, and a Belgian Malinois named Duvel.

For more information about Larissa, visit www.larissaione.com.

Discover More Larissa Ione

Razr: A Demonica Novella by Larissa Ione, Now Available

A fallen angel with a secret.

An otherworldly elf with an insatiable hunger she doesn't understand.

An enchanted gem.

Meet mortal enemies Razr and Jedda...and the priceless diamond that threatens to destroy them both even as it bonds them together with sizzling passion.

Welcome back to the Demonica Underworld, where enemies find love...if they're strong enough to survive.

* * * *

Azagoth: A Demonica Underword Novella by Larissa Ione, Now Available

Even in the fathomless depths of the underworld and the bleak chambers of a damaged heart, the bonds of love can heal...or destroy.

He holds the ability to annihilate souls in the palm of his hand. He commands the respect of the most dangerous of demons and the most powerful of angels. He can seduce and dominate any female he wants with a mere look. But for all Azagoth's power, he's bound by shackles of his own making, and only an angel with a secret holds the key to his release.

She's an angel with the extraordinary ability to travel through time and space. An angel with a tormented past she can't escape. And when Lilliana is sent to Azagoth's underworld realm, she finds that her past isn't all she can't escape. For the irresistibly sexy fallen angel known as

Azagoth is also known as the Grim Reaper, and when he claims a soul, it's forever...

* * * *

Hades: A Demonica Underworld Novella by Larissa Ione, Now Available

A fallen angel with a mean streak and a mohawk, Hades has spent thousands of years serving as Jailor of the Underworld. The souls he guards are as evil as they come, but few dare to cross him. All of that changes when a sexy fallen angel infiltrates his prison and unintentionally starts a riot. It's easy enough to quell an uprising, but for the first time, Hades is torn between delivering justice — or bestowing mercy — on the beautiful female who could be his salvation...or his undoing.

Thanks to her unwitting participation in another angel's plot to start Armageddon, Cataclysm was kicked out of Heaven and is now a fallen angel in service of Hades's boss, Azagoth. All she wants is to redeem herself and get back where she belongs. But when she gets trapped in Hades's prison domain with only the cocky but irresistible Hades to help her, Cat finds that where she belongs might be in the place she least expected...

* * * *

Z: A Demonica Underworld Novella by Larissa Ione, Now Available

Zhubaal, fallen angel assistant to the Grim Reaper, has spent decades searching for the angel he loved and lost nearly a century ago. Not even her death can keep him from trying to find her, not when he knows she's been given a second chance at life in a new body. But as time passes, he's losing hope, and he wonders how much longer he can hold to the oath he swore to her so long ago...

As an *emim*, the wingless offspring of two fallen angels, Vex has always felt like a second-class citizen. But if she manages to secure a deal with the Grim Reaper — by any means necessary — she will have earned her place in the world. The only obstacle in the way of her plan is a sexy hardass called Z, who seems determined to thwart her at every turn. Soon it becomes clear that they have a powerful connection rooted in the past…but can any vow stand the test of time?

On behalf of 1001 Dark Nights,

Liz Berry and M.J. Rose would like to thank ~

Steve Berry
Doug Scofield
Kim Guidroz
Jillian Stein
InkSlinger PR
Dan Slater
Asha Hossain
Chris Graham
Fedora Chen
Kasi Alexander
Jessica Johns
Dylan Stockton
Richard Blake
BookTrib After Dark
and Simon Lipskar

18309714R00118

Made in the USA
Middletown, DE
30 November 2018